# CHALLENGE

R.E. Korns

R.E. Korns

# CHALLENGE

Published by

## WORTHGOLD PUBLISHING

17415 Mayerling St.
Granada Hills, CA 91344

The publisher and author wish to thank Kirk Thomas, Lucinda Red, Steven Horwich and especially my wife Carol Worthey for their assistance in reviewing, editing and preparing this book for publication. Your help is appreciated.!

Cover Artwork: "Capitol City" by Raymond E. Korns
Copyright © 2016 Raymond E. Korns

Library of Congress Control Number: 2016pending
ISBN: 978-0-6923520-9-0
Printed in the United States of America

www.Worthgold.com

R.E. Korns

# CONTENTS

## Table of Contents

# AUTHOR PREAMBLE

In the summer of 2006 I had an inspiration for a short science-fiction story and in a flurry of activity set down the basis of this tale. I had wanted to create the type of science-fiction that I so relished as a child reading the great authors of the 'Golden Age'. I have read some fantastic new works by the great and upcoming authors who are keeping the genre alive, but their stories too often leave me — as a reader — cold and unfulfilled as with a great technological polish, nevertheless they lacked a certain "humanity" or humanistic viewpoint regarding the future and "irony" about the present.

Unfortunately, time and Life intervened to put my project on the back-burner — for a while not even on a 'simmer' setting. Returning to the project in 2011 I realized that to do the story justice, it would have to be a much longer creation. Thanks to the encouragement of my wife, Carol Worthey, and author and friend Steven David Horwich I pushed ahead. Then in 2013 everything was "almost ready" when Life again intervened! At last, everything is fully cooked and you are now in possession of the final result, a story which I like and I hope you will very much enjoy.

— R.E. Korns, May 2016

R.E. Korns

# CHAPTER ONE

## Prologue

Head bowed, not really watching where his small feet landed, Fen walked near the curb of the hot Capital street. The Dactoes sun fell over his shoulder and warmed his neck. He squinted his eyes from the bright glare of sunlight on the concrete sidewalk.

The fair Charin had rejected him utterly, Krek's gang had taunted and ridiculed him mercilessly, teasing him about his thick glasses with their ugly black frames. How had he come to this pass?

How could he happily live with such fools? Did they actually think he was the little body that appeared before them at prison school each day?

Stumbling on a crack in the pavement, Fen fell and scraped his knee tearing a small hole in his left pants leg. "Damn!" Fen thought, "They'll think I was fighting again when they see this." The only fighting Fen ever did was to fend off blows while being beaten to a pulp by the (much) older contingent of Krek's buddies.

To his right stretching past the hot shimmering concrete of the roadway an unkept, weed-infested field extended into the distance. To his left hot wind devils were blowing upward from

3

"the pit." The "pit" was an old quarry that had been graded and seeded and turned into a crude exercise ground for Fen's school. A great cloud of dust teared Fen's eyes.

Seemingly from within, Fen heard laughter, not kids' laughter but a deep, cruel kind of laughter with more than a hint of disdain. Looking up through his tearing eyes, Fen rubbed the dust from his lenses, taking care not to pull apart the frame where it was taped (after Krek "accidentally" sat on them).

Blocking his way down the hill was an almost-visible apparition. It appeared to be a distortion in the air hiding something solid. The air shimmered already from the hot concrete, but this was quite different. The distortion seemed to coalesce like pieces of gelatin submerged in water, hard to see, yet definitely there. The laughter continued, emanating from the distortion that was now straight ahead in his path.

Memory returned, Fen knew this. He yanked himself from his well of despair and looked hard. Placing the thought "Get out of my way!" directly into the distortion, Fen unconsciously planted his small feet in a defense posture. This action caused the emanation to issue a more grating laughter in response.

Fen looked around to see if anyone else heard this, but he was completely alone on the deserted street. More memories seemed to activate and with a surprisingly intense resolve, again he placed the thought into the distortion and this time said aloud as well: "Get out of my way!" straight into the heart of the taunt. The laughter ceased.

A somehow not-entirely-unexpected blast of force hit him squarely in the chest. If Fen had not been instinctively prepared, he would have been knocked flat on his back. His glasses fell from his face yet his eyes cleared and (if he could have seen it) radiated a steel blue intensity completely unknown in his nine-year tenure on this world.

Now Fen could focus clearly on the burning, churning creature that blocked his way. "Get the hell out of my way, fiend!" he said under his breath, redoubling his intention. The distortion began to fade, finally fading completely with a lame "pop" but the words "...you'll be sorry..." grew inside his head as if hissing from the hot, swirling wind.

Picking up his glasses from the dust, Fen disgustedly stuffed them into a pocket and continued walking home. But he forgot to forget.

# CHAPTER TWO

## Unexpected

Fen's teenage mind wandered as he endured yet another painful, wasted afternoon in yet another wasted year in prison school. For at least the last five years he could not shrug the feeling that somehow he was "being watched" although nothing significant had become of it. Still, he sensed a kind of dangerousness to his situation. "There's really nothing I should be worrying about," he thought.

There were about twenty kids in Fen's "Upper" classroom. They were the same twenty kids Fen had grown up with all his life. Charin, a year younger than Fen, sat aloof near the front corner of the room near the windows surreptitiously filing her nails while the prim, petite literature teacher Miss Turpante droned meaninglessly on and on from the other side of the room. Turpante's hair was tied tightly back on her head — decades out-of-style.

Fen gazed at Charin (his only real interest in the room) across the heads of the other students from the opposite corner near the door. Realizing that Charin had noticed him and was getting annoyed, Fen forced himself to stop staring at her and turned his gaze to the left.

Idly he noticed his friends Lall and Nar clearly dozing. Lall, eyes closed, was resting his chin on his hand as his elbow and arm propped up his head (trying not to snore). Lall's cherub-like face with its angelic look and straw-colored hair was totally out of proportion to his large shoulders and athletic chest. Lall looked somewhat like a middle-weight wrestler whose head had been squeezed by an opponent into a too-small grape then his rosy-cheeked face painted on. Nar had given up totally and his slumped head lay on his desk curled in his arm. While slightly more feline in his countenance, Nar could have been Lall's siamese twin brother. Indeed, not only did the two look alike but they were inseparable, had the same likes and dislikes and now were both asleep together. They had been Fen's neighbors and playmates when younger, but they had become more distant as Fen grew older and had become more and more interested in mathematics, an interest they were not mentally equipped to share.

In front of Fen sat another friend, Gem. In contrast to Lall and Nar, Gem was thin, pimply and fragile-looking with dark hair. Gem had the reputation for being a "brain". Contemplative and introverted Gem was typically nervous when around even a few others, especially girls. Gem would only intellectually become engaged with Fen when debating technical subjects, otherwise Fen had a distinct feeling Gem was uncomfortable in his presence. Gem was part of Upper's Tech-Team and was clearly being pushed toward a technical career.    Thankfully, the back of Gem's head conveniently blocked Fen's view of Turpante as Fen slouched in his seat.

Fen gazed down on his desk at the fat, propped-up Literature volume and saw the thin smaller algebra book he had secreted within, its glaring quadratic equations containing a complex proof clearly printed on an open page.  With his tired eyes the equations appeared to him to be dancing patterns across the pages.

Looking up from the book, he sighed. Scanning further to his left, Fen caught glimpses of other covert activity. Krek, the class bully, sat in the back by the window in the last row (and too close to Charin for Fen) stretching his too-long legs into the aisle.  Krek was secreting a "sexy" magazine within *his* propped-up Literature book.  He had a smirk on his dark acne-pockmarked face but was hiding it from Turpante with his hand in front of his mouth.   Turpante noticed nothing of this and continued to drone on about great Literature's *absolute* subservience to State politics.

Retreating into his own universe, Fen thought dreamily of possibilities. Fen and Charin sitting close together on a blanket in the shade, the warm breeze slightly fragrant as it stroked Charin's face pushing back her long, brown hair revealing her lovely olive-green eyes.  It was not the real Charin, but the dream Charin who was somehow older and eager to ask Fen all about mathematics and science and waited excitedly upon Fen's every word, her lovely breasts slowly heaving with her shortened, excited breath and...

As she droned, Turpante had slowly been walking down the side of the classroom toward where Fen was seated.

"Fen! What is this?" chirped an angry Miss Turpante, breaking his reverie and grabbing the algebra paper as she spotted it from within his book. Finding the paper to be algebra she looked somewhat disappointed because it was not a major infraction that would require strict detention and punishment.

"Hah!" petite Miss Turpante snorted in a voice not quite her own as looking up at Fen she roughly pushed him from his seat to the floor. As he sat on the floor, the startled class — now laughing and happy for the distraction — jockeyed for better positions from which to view Fen's discomfiture.

Fen looked into Turpante's dark, black, glazed eyes (not at all normal). As Fen watched, Miss Turpante's face seemed to waver, distort and coalese into a mask. The room itself seemed to haze and shimmer like a heat wave rising from asphalt in the sun. Turpante's jaw slacked in an open-mouthed gape and now from within a deep, scratchy, guttural voice hissed: "Get out of my way!"

A vague voice recognition gave Fen only a moment to jump out of the way of Miss Turpante's ferocious kick which slammed his desk into the wall a full ten feet away barely missing his friend Gem who leaped out of the desk's path with a surprised, anxious look.

The class was not laughing now. Fen was barely fast enough to scramble out of the way as Miss Turpante's foot came down on the floor with a "KRAK!" so hard it broke the heel of her shoe and dented the floor where just a second before his thigh had been.

Thara, the red-headed girl who sat behind Fen sprang to her feet and emitted a shriek. Fen rolled, got to his feet and (firmly pushing Thara aside) sprinted for the door. Miss Turpante beat him to it, but fortunately Fen slipped on the wood floor just as Turpante drove her left fist with enormous force through the plaster wall just above his head.

When she yanked her hand from the wall, the force of the blow had driven her long painted fingernails into her palm cutting it. A small trickle of blood ran down her arm dripping from the flowered bracelet she wore as she prepared to strike again.

Fen was badly shaken. Pulling back from daydreaming he mustered his wits. New strength coursed through him, memories flashed as if preprogrammed equations were activated. He knew. He knew who he was. He knew where he was. He recognized her. "Stand down!" he loudly commanded Turpante, falling instinctively into a defense posture. Instantly Turpante dropped, crumpled to the floor, barely breathing.

He had never touched her. "What the hell?" he thought.

The school sorted it out. The Principal Leader (encouraged by a helpful Krek) clearly recognized that Fen had viciously attacked Miss Turpante for discovering the pornographic magazine Fen had hidden in his book. Although Miss Turpante had been hospitalized in a foaming fit, she had declined to name Fen her attacker, therefore the hole in the wall "proved" Fen's attack and there was no further questioning. Fen had been fighting again and he had already been warned. This time he was lucky — he was only detained and confined.

# CHAPTER THREE

## Confined

Fen stood at rigid attention following rollcall while Group Leader Lars in his steel-gray uniform loped along the long row of detainees. Stopping to sneer at Fen, Lars barked in his face: "You're in Dog Corps! Forget about Upper, you're a sleeb and you're mine!" Lars had done this to Fen everyday at First Check for the last six months. Lars was a straight-faced, scheming man, square-jawed, muscular and long-limbed. He was older and heavier than any in Dog Corps and had worked his way up the ranks by stepping on, extorting or bribing all who stood in the way of his advancement with his superiors. Fortunately now Fen had assimilated enough of Lars personality traits that Fen could usually negotiate a course other than "target" for the rest of the day. The operational principle of Dog Corps was vendetta and everything to do with living became a potential offense.

"There's crap to be done in Capital today," Lars mused loudly, "...and you're the ones who will do it!" Oddly, Fen's reputation as a hair-trigger violent was his primary protection from the many martinets like Lars in the Dog Corps leadership, but there was none worse than Lars. The Corps deliberately had no insignia, except perhaps for the gray and black, usually dirty, jumpsuits that they were required to wear.

Lars had reached Krek and was chewing him out for a small tear in a back pocket of his coverlet. "Smell my breath, hear my words!" he yelled directly in Krek's ear. Fen might have smiled if he had not been at attention.

Krek, of course, was delighted with Fen's fall from Upper until he himself "joined" Dog Corps later. Caught in one of his many indiscretions he was put where some, in spite of Krek's clan connections, said he belonged. Although personally a coward, and publicly treated harshly by Lars, Krek had become the perfect lap-dog and informer for Lars in private. Krek's arrival created real stress for Fen as he now daily had to defend himself from Krek's constant insults and constant invitation to fight back.

"Heave to!" Lars commanded and the line of bodies shoved and pushed into a long line by two's and Dog Corps shuffled to the first class of the morning as a group. As Dog Corps filed past a small group of Upper, Fen saw Preed, one of his former friends, and nodded. Preed, large and solidly built with the close-cropped hair of the Genna clan, was an unusual blend of thoughtfulness combined with physical strength. Preed was the kind of personality that disliked discord and sought to remedy situations. Fen had admired him greatly when still in Upper. But Fen's supposed "friend" conveniently turned his back, pretending not to notice as Fen shuffled past.

Farther down the hallway, Fen spied Charin standing next to an Upper classroom door. She was wearing a peach-colored, flowered print dress that emphasized her long hair. She was looking directly at him with fire in her eyes following his movement down the hallway. "Is she trying to communicate something to me?" Fen thought. Unable to help himself Fen smiled appreciatively. Her look changed to neutral immediately and she shook her head as if saying "No." "Hummmpf!" she uttered under her breath with pursed lips as he passed. Fen turned his back to her so she would not see his pained look.

It was not the injustice of his summary sentence that annoyed Fen, but the fact that not one of his supposed friends took care to volunteer any true account of the Turpante incident.

Another day rolled on and on. Between the Obedience classes and the Loyalty classes were the interminable physical tasks that Dog Corps was assigned. Late in the day, Fen lined up at attention with the others for Last Check.

"Break Out!" Lars commanded and the line of bodies relaxed and yelling, pushing and taunting, moved mechanically to the night pen. Fen walked wearily following them, counting the days until age alone would release him from this bondage.

Fen's supposed "violent nature" had inadvertently earned him one boon: He was locked-up separately in night pen. It was not much, but he did not have to endure barracks and the pranks and small cruelties that were a constant there. It allowed him a rare opportunity to be alone and think. Fen reasoned the school administration only did this out of fear. Dog Corps contained the refuse, the delinquents and incalcitrant of the system. What if a "Loyal Clan son" who had somehow fallen from Upper, (temporarily it was hoped) like Krek, to the depths of Dog Corps were found some night strangled to death in barracks, a victim of the evil offspring from a Rebel Clan – like Fen! They weren't taking any chances.

Waiting until he was sure there would be no inspection tonight, Fen retrieved from hiding the few personal items he had saved before being confined. A diffused beacon-like light from a full Mother Moon streamed through the high slitted windows at a thirty degree angle like bright white knives slicing the black floor of his cell.

Fen held the crumpled picture of his mother in an oblong pool of light and gazed sadly at it. He had only one word with his mother in public before being marched into confinement. Fen had just said "Sorry."

"Prison school," he said softly to the dark empty air with an ironic smile. That's what his family had always called it in private and it had become that in truth for him.

Despite the long intervening years since the rebellion, the fact that Fen's great paternal grandfather (after whom he had been named) had been an executed rebel leader was not lost on either the school administration nor the students. Each morning the Roll of Loyal Clans was called. Students from loyalist families would rise while Fen would sit. Notably, most of Dog Corps remained seated which simply reasserted their isolation. There would be no reconciliation while these policies continued to keep the old enmities alive for each new generation.

Fen missed his father.

When Fen's dad was alive he would occasionally coax his father to talk about the rebellion (a punishable offense). Fen's mother remained close-lipped and tense whenever the subject was even slightly brushed. It was his mom's influence that had originally gotten Fen into Upper.

"It wasn't even a rebellion... it was just a protest," Fen's dad had said. "My grandfather Fen always promoted discussion and disavowed violence, when others would have taken arms. After The Suppression, things changed... Kill Corps was created."

Fen's generation had been told that Kill Corps had been disbanded and as a group folded into the military, but the military, the domestic police and everybody else still seemed to take orders from anyone wearing the scarlet red uniform. The red uniform was still called Kill Corps and universally feared even though they no longer wore the "crossed-hooks" insignia. Troublesome people seemed to just "disappear" from time to time. The black pods were still sometimes visible at the edge of the hazy sky during the early morning and late evening slowly moving in two long lines from horizon to horizon – just like in the old days.

The only positive thing that had come from detainment was that Fen had no more need of glasses. To his astonishment, the enforced heavy exercise and dark confinement had somehow changed and improved his eyesight. Fen's lean physique had also filled out and he had become quite athletic. He had been surprised to overhear a classmate refer to him and his movements as "panther-like".

Fen carefully replaced the picture of his mom into the shallow box which he hid in a crack at the bottom of the wall, taking care not to look at the small picture of Charin over which he placed it.

# CHAPTER FOUR

## In A Daze

"What the hell is taking you so long in there?" Charin whispered furtively into the dark hole where Fen had disappeared. Child Moon's pale light as it had filtered through the constant wave clouds already had faded as it set. This began the dark period, or "Dark", that occurred only once every sixty-two days. They had already been here ten minutes and in less than an hour Mother Moon would rise like a diffused searchlight giving a radiance almost like daylight.

Looking up at the hole, where the anxious Charin peered down on him, he said as loud as he dared, "Count down the remaining *time* for me — every ten minutes."

As he briefly looked up at her, Charin's head was haloed in the oval port opening by the slightly lighter sky behind her from the surrounding black mat of the interior. Charin always looked lovely to him. She had a determined, mature look that did not match her seventeen years.

"I missed something the last time we were here..." Fen thought to himself as he poked around the wrecked pod directing the beam from his stolen wrist-torch from side to side by pointing his outstretched fist, "...and I'm missing something in the records."

While he searched, Fen started to mentally string together the precipitous events that led him and Charin to this wrecked craft....

* * *

He started secretly meeting with Charin after Dog Corps had been forced to repair part of the school basement, normally off-limits. There under a moldy pile of records lay a tattered journal-of-proceedings. Time seemed suspended. Even in the basement gloom the cover title seemed emblazoned: *"CONFIDENTIAL — Turpante Inquiry."* It was marked Archive 2, definitely misplaced to have ended up in the basement. "Unlikely ever to be missed," he reasoned. He knew he had to take it regardless of risk.

He found distorted classmate affidavits within the journal pages. Charin's report had been the only one accurately describing what had happened. She had been accused of lying and censured for coming to his defense. If she were seen with Fen, or even spoke with him, she would be confined. Administratively Charin was to be shuffled to a "useless" profession, like archeology or poetry and married as soon as she was of age.

Knowing factually that Charin had been formally censured had given Fen an enormous sense of relief. It confirmed what he always knew, that as much as he had wanted to see and talk to

Charin, it would have somehow put her in danger. Maybe there was still some hope of getting together with her after his release from Dog Corps after turning eighteen this year! Fen wondered had any of his other former friends been pressured to shun him because of the example made of Charin, or was it just Dog Corps?

On the last page of the report he found his own official damnation:

**Disciplinary Advocate Findings - Turpante Incident**

**Fen Dathrod of Clan Grem, being found guilty of disruption, is to be detained. He will be confined within Dog Corps under strict supervision until his eighteenth birthday. He may at that time be permitted to apply for a post. He is to be permanently limited to no higher than Labor 2 Grade. Under NO circumstances is he to be permitted to any access or training in Tech ranks.**

**Tapa Dathrod of Clan Grem, being guilty of raising a disrupter, is to be transported to Tarpin as accessory to disruption. All her property is forfeit and herein confiscated. She is to remain a minor dependent of Farid Probid of Clan Grek.**

No communication is permitted between Tapa and the offender Fen. Any additional disruption will result in Chambers.

Signed, Roff, Advocate Governor.

Note to Frake: Given Fen's innocent appearance and his tendency to violent outburst, see if he can be recruited to your branch. Consider termination if you cannot get compliance.

So... his mother Tapa was to be sent to his uncle Farid, a minor clan functionary on Tarpin, an island two-hundred clicks to the south. This was worse than Fen's own confinement as her hated half-brother would insure that the clan dishonor of her deportment would never be forgotten or forgiven.

The reference to Chambers had sobered and chilled him. Chambers was an inquisitional ordeal where people just vanished, or if released, were unable to talk about it.

Who was the sinister Frake anyway?

* * *

"Fifty minutes to moon rise.....," Charin whispered from above as Fen re-examined the far end of the pod.

* * *

The same afternoon he had found the proceedings journal and absorbed the gist of it, he took a grim look at his future prospects, IF he made it through school.

"Fool!" he thought to himself as soon as he read the journal. He now realized Charin had tried for years to create safe opportunities for them to speak. Stupidly or pridefully he had assumed she wished to taunt him or lure him into betraying his feelings.

"I *must* find out as much as possible from the rest of the basement records and whatever Charin knows," he mused, "or I haven't one chance in hell!" He decided to tackle questioning Charin for more information. This would be his first priority.

* * *

"Forty minutes to moon rise....," whispered Charin from above.

Fen tried to think faster and move faster, continually playing his wrist-torch back and forth. "What am I missing?" he thought.

* * *

Hurrying – before the basement repairs were completed – Fen discovered a forgotten alcove by the food dispensers and waited for Charin. "Shhhhh!" he whispered, as she walked out of the eatery, as he put his hand over her mouth and pulled her into the alcove.

"You oaf!" were her first words to him when they were finally alone and he released her. "I've been keeping a message from your mother for the last four years!!!"

"I know she's in Tarpin," Fen had countered.

"You *know?* Your mom made me *promise* to tell you she would *not* stay with Farid. She's in Reem with his daughter Lurr."

She sensed Fen's relief at the news but was surprised at his knowledge. Huddled in the small space, they managed to talk undiscovered for three hours straight as he filled her in on what he had learned. Charin treated him with more respect after that.

"I'm... well... sorry I misread you," he said in a quiet, broken voice grabbing her arm as she turned to go.

"I don't have any friends except... oddly, you!" Charin whispered, hiding her face as she left.

* * *

"Thirty minutes to moon rise... please hurry up!" whispered Charin.

* * *

After that first meeting, they had agreed to undertake the task of searching the basement archive together. It had been easier than either had expected. Fen had deliberately violated one of Lars many rules and had been punitively assigned night-duty to "guard" the in-progress repairs. Charin, being part of the Upper, already a Tech 3 grade, (and a woman) was mostly ignored. Staying in late-evening at Terminal, she could be absent unnoticed for hours. By using Charin's scan cube (forbidden to Fen) they were relieved to obtain copies without having to steal them.

To their astonishment, they found data on the rebellion. There was a crashed pod revealed to them through a transcript:

"Chamber Interrogatory 301993b

**Quisit:** Pod Group Leader Targ, is it true you violated X space?"

**Targ:** Yes sir, that is correct.

**Quisit:** What do you have to say in your defense?

**Targ:** I violated X space only to engage the rebel pod.

**Quisit:** What rebel pod? Continental defense reported no pod!

**Targ:** A Grem rebel pod, invisible on scan approached us visually requesting a parley.

**Quisit:** Where was this?

**Targ:** Grid 6, coordinate B in X space. Our altitude was low, about 3 clicks below wave cloud boundary.

**Quisit:** You are aware that any parley action with rebels is considered as disruption do you not? You are also aware that all Grem leaders have been terminated and the clan thirds detained.

**Targ:** Yes sir.

**Quisit:** What did you do?

**Targ:** I set a trap for them and when they were fully in range, I believe I personally fired for their tubes.

**Quisit:** You BELIEVE you fired?

**Targ:** Yes sir, I had to actually shoot two of the crew to prevent them from trying to parley. I was very disoriented for a time, but I distinctly recall throwing the firing switch.

**Quisit:** And what was the result?

**Targ:** They went down sir. We were, however, too close and sustained a type five failure ourselves. I received only minor injuries, two of my crew are in hospital, two were shot and the remaining three were killed on impact.

**Quisit:** What proof have you of your actions?

**Targ:** The proof Sir would be our characteristic burn pattern on the rebel hull.

**Quisit:** What I think... Sir... is YOU are a liar! You have no recordings. There was no rebel ship. Grem is neutralized. YOU are the rebel and this was all a ruse to violate X space. Do you think we are all incompetent fools?

**Targ:** (no comment)"

A short note attached to the transcript stated:

"Re: **X Space Incursion**
To: Clan Advocate
Targ and the other two traitors in hospital have been terminated. Should their ashes be returned to their families as state war heroes, or are their names to be posted on the rebel lists?
-Frake, Kill Corps"

It had been one hundred twenty-two years since the pods had crashed, but Charin was a brilliant detective and plotted out not only where the crashed rebel pod probably was, but that it might still be there because Planetary believed it never existed!

Fen was confused. He was Grem. His mother was Grem. He had never heard of any thirds having been detained. It was nowhere in the clan history. Charin's maternal grandmother had been Grem but unusually married out-of-clan making Charin part Grem. Had he been deliberately targeted? His answer might lie within the rebel pod.

The ominous Frake had not approached Fen to recruit him. Fen had turned eighteen and had been released from prison school. He immediately applied for permission to train as a Tech 4 (which was expected and was of course denied) and was given a lowly Labor 4 designation.

\* \* \*

"Twenty minutes to moon rise... hurry!!"

A helmeted human skull shone momentarily in the beam of Fen's wrist-torch... the crew had never escaped. "What am I missing?" he thought.

\* \* \*

The rebel pod had gone down in Tarf, a hot-spot during the rebellion but now a pock-marked, bomb-cratered rural area largely un-repopulated.

Fen easily had obtained a Tarf Labor 4 post under the misspelled name "Fendath Rod". It was only part-time and gave him plenty of free time as well as migrants' housing. He developed a reputation as "lazy" and his work-team let him know how expendable he was by seldom calling him to work. However, whenever there was a particularly onerous job he was summoned.

For her last school year Charin obtained a long-term Archeology permit for a solo research trip. "Loyal-clan Ancients" was to be the title of her paper. She would take over the abandoned work at an isolated prehistoric site, totally unimportant but near their search area. A rustic shed with camping facilities had been built into the side of a large mound and equiped for use on the site.

Due to the heavy labor he was assigned, Fen had filled-out and become physically fit and so was able to hollow out several secret rooms in the rock-hard clay behind the shed, one behind the other. He hid there most days when possible and by night, searched....

"I've found it! The pod!" Charin said, shaking Fen in the early afternoon as he lay asleep after a particularly grueling work shift.

The buried surface had gleamed a shiny black when they brushed the dirt from part of the hull. A nearby explosion had apparently completely covered the craft hiding it with a foot-deep layer of dirt.

He was now approaching his nineteenth birthday. It took four months of probing to find the entry port. Ironically, the entry was high up, so they did not have to dig deep to access the port – finding it was a birthday present. Opening it up meant having to wait for a Dark, otherwise the opened port would be exposed to red scanners and possible discovery. (During the rebellion, because the infrequent Darks seldom lasted more than an hour, scanners were permanently installed on Dactoes moons instead of full close-orbit coverage.)

* * *

Clenching his fist, Fen worried, "What *have* I missed?  Tonight is the last Dark for another sixty-two days!"

"Ten minutes to moon rise!!!!!!" came Charin's urgent voice from above.

Fen suddenly had a thought: "The red scanners!  What do they key on?"

It had to be something that would be active *in* the pod when the port was open.  *That* was the danger, *that* was what they had missed!

Quickly turning off his wrist-light he blinked and strained his eyes.

"What the hell are you doing?" Charin said above him thrusting her head into the port.

After his eyes adjusted, there, not five feet from where he stood he saw a pale green glow. Aiming his fist at it in the dark he turned on his wrist-light.  There, buried under the dust and debris of an overturned and broken rack was a very large box.  Brushing off the dust with his glove he saw the box was an active port-a-console.  He had seen it many times in his earlier search but never realized its significance. It looked as if the rack had protected it – amazingly powered all these years as if waiting for them to discover it.

Fen grabbed the cube from his pocket and scanned the console closely, then scrambled out the port. "Grab here!" Together they strained to close the ancient hatch. Camouflaging the slight depression with a light layer of dirt and some underbrush, he and Charin retreated to safety as the night sky started to lighten rapidly.

It would be sixty-two days but they would plan and be back to "rescue" the console.

# CHAPTER FIVE

## Visitor

Muscles bulging, Fen picked up the heavy rack and giving it a shove freed the large console. Fen watched as Charin skillfully opened a side access panel using the instructions obtained from a dusty, previously salvaged craft manual and disabled the ID transponder. The green indicator that he had first seen went off and a yellow indicator turned on.

"There," she said finishing, "now we don't have to wait until a Dark to examine more of the wreck."

The next day Charin had approached the Labor Boss in the nearby town where Fen worked. "I need a single day laborer part-time," she asked, "it's very, very heavy, very dirty work."

"I have just the man for you," the Labor Boss smiled at her as he pulled Fendath's duty card from a file.

Fen "Fendath" officially reported for work the next day.

Charin's prehistoric "research trip" cover and Fendath's help allowed her to be seen hauling objects in and out of the shed without suspicion. Having full access to the wreck, the first thing they did was to remove and secret the console in the corner of the inner hidden room. Charin could now study and activate the console mechanisms and retrieve data from its database. In the following days they discovered and removed many more rebel artifacts than Fen's original superficial surveys had revealed.

* * *

"You have never looked so lovely," Group Leader Lars said to Charin in a snidely-sweet, uncharacteristic voice. He appeared out of nowhere walking past a shallow trench toward the mound of dirt on which Charin stood. She wore a frayed yellow sun hat and had to squint into the sun to recognize him.

Shocked at his unexpected arrival, she coldly replied, "What are you doing here and what do you want?"

"I have a few days leave and I really felt I needed to see more of the countryside." Lars' lie was transparent — he cared nothing for things pastoral.

"I have chores to do and can't waste time talking," she said turning her back to him and picking up the nearest pot-shard she spied. Fen was due to return at any minute! Her heart pounded as she rummaged through the dirt pretending to look for more shards. "Watch out! Watch out!" she thought urgently, shaping her thoughts like a broadcast.

It worked. Fen seemed to sense Charin's feelings. Cautiously turning the corner of the shed, he saw the back of Lars' steel-gray Group Leader uniform and quickly ducked back.

"You shouldn't have to do all the heavy work alone. You should let me help you," Lars offered.

"I am quite capable of handling my own research work thank you," she countered, heart still pounding.

"Such important work too, it really ought to be better supported, especially for such a charming woman as you!" Lars added condescendingly.

Despite Lars tailing her like some stalking cat, Fen finally managed to signal to her that he was aware of the situation, much to Charin's relief.

That night from his cot in the inner hidden room Fen cautioned her. "He's probably here to check up and report on you. You'll have to appear very busy." Then he thought to himself "He's got his own private agenda... with you."

"I can handle that jerk," she had said biting her lip.

Fen wondered if she'd read his mind.

Lars remained for a week. Charin stayed very cool to Lars but was quite annoyed at having to pick up pot shards and bric-a-brac carting them back to the shed for "analysis" while Lars dogged her heels and flattered her with ridiculous compliments that were really more veiled insults.

Lars made no headway and got tired of the game, especially after Charin had him spend an entire day from dawn past dusk hoisting filthy pots from the ancient site and carting them to the shed, staining and tearing his proud steel-gray uniform.

"Once you return to Capital," Lars said departing, "we'll talk. I've been offered a fantastic post and I'm taking it. I've also had some words with your father and I expect him to tender an offer."

Charin blanched. She realized that if her father offered her in marriage to Lars and Lars accepted before her eighteenth birthday, as chattel under the old law she could be forced to accept Lars or go to court. It would be a clan black mark if she were to refuse her father's choice of husband. Involuntarily she shuddered.

"Is he gone?" Fen asked when she found him covered in clay head-to-toe later that afternoon.

"Finally!" she groaned, mentioning nothing about the offer.

A smile appeared through Fen's mask of clay.

Charin laughed, "What in hell have you been doing?"

"I've used the time to enlarge our accommodations. When Lars showed up I realized we could be trapped here. So I've dug several escape tunnels. I'm afraid he'll be back...."

# CHAPTER SIX

## Finding Out

Charin looked up from her work. "It must be past the middle of the night," she thought adjusting the mini-light above the makeshift desk. She had worked the console database decryption keys a dozen ways but made no progress. Perhaps if she tried a section that should be clear she could determine the data sequencing used for the encrypted part.

The mini cast a shadow across the room to the other side where Fen lay snoring slightly. "He's really counting on me to break the database seals," she brooded, blinking her tired eyes. "If only I hadn't brushed-off Podro at school," she mused.

Podro had been a Tech 1 and completely boring to her but she knew he'd be able to crack open this database. She remembered his excited conversation trying to interest her in the subtle beauties of data storage. Forcing herself, she recalled his voice. "If the four levels are present, then three is always the clear," Podro had said. Returning with renewed intensity to her task, she plotted level three.

An entire sequence of recordings fell out into clear and she had limited access. She had now recovered the pod's last audio logs before its doom. Deciding against waking Fen, she retired to her own cot to rest, letting the mini burn as a night-light relieving the perpetual gloom of their subterranean hideaway.

"I've cracked a piece of it," she told him the next morning as they chewed protein sticks and sat on a bench in front of the shed.

"Why didn't you wake me!?" he exclaimed.

"You needed the rest and... I'm not sure I want to know," she confided, "It's the last audio logs before the crash."

The sun rose slowly in the sky piercing below the wave cloud barrier for some minutes revealing two faint lines of slow moving black dots. Fen and Charin sat together, not speaking, until the sun and the dots faded into obscurity within the cloud cover. Without a word Fen followed Charin into the shed and behind a hinged panel and down into the outer hidden chamber.

"Who are you?" the voice said out of the console once Charin started playing the log.

"Fen of Grem and requesting a parley," came the reply. Fen gasped — it was the voice of his namesake, his great-grandfather. So it wasn't true. He had never been captured and executed as Fen had been told as a child!

"Targ of Senior Corps does not speak to rebels and traitors. Why aren't you on our screens?" came the quick reply.

"Never mind the screens, you parley with me, Targ. I bring proof of Upper Council's treachery against Senior Corps and news that will affect Dactoes for a thousand years," Fen's great-grandfather said.

"Why should I risk everything to listen to you?" Targ replied.

"Does 'Racktar Plen' mean anything to you?" snapped great-grandfather Fen.

"Parley granted, scramble circuit six," came Targ's instant reply.

It was eerie hearing the recordings of long dead voices as they debated the fate of an entire world.

"We're secure.... How do you know about Racktar?" There was an awkward pause while the crew switched channels, then Targ's voice came back.

At first, under their temporary truce, pod leader Targ had queried and listened intently as great-grandfather Fen had begun to explain the sources of their intelligence, but then Targ's voice had started to distort. It was as if each time the name 'Racktar' was mentioned Targ's voice would fluctuate and blur and become almost indistinguishable for a moment.

"You tell me you are aware of the Racktar thousand-year plan for the future of Dactoes. Do you believe it? Don't you understand that it's not just *our* clan to be destroyed but *all* clans?" Fen's great-grandfather had said to Targ.

Now there were clear sounds of a crew struggle coming from Targ's pod....

"Too close – Don't!" said another voice from Targ's pod.

A scream came from one of Targ's crew and the unmistakable sound of a snap-stick firing.

"What's going on there?" said a voice from the rebel pod's crew.

"Traitor – Fiend! Release that switch..." said yet another of Targ's crew as again the "braaaaakkkkk!" of a snap-stick was heard.

"Break off contact!" ordered Fen's great-grandfather.

Targ uttered one word like two voices overlayed: "Dieeeee!!!" hissed from his lips like a hot wind.

The tearing, rending screech that followed seemed interminable, then abruptly ended in a shattering silence. Both Charin and Fen felt their teeth vibrating from the shock as they sat, silent and motionless in front of the quiet console, their hands sweating too much to turn a dial.

A change came over them. They both realized it had been a grand adventure until now. Their whole histories were wrapped up in a rebellion and a plot that had never ended. More than just *their* lives were at stake.

It was now crucial to crack into the rebel database.

# CHAPTER SEVEN

## Disaster

They had been careless.

From the moment Fen had heard 'Racktar Plen' memories had stirred within him. It was as if (at the sound of those two potent words) a switch had been "turned on." Indefinite shadows of people and places pulsed through his thoughts like flashes of scenes from an old showvid. Were these real? He had no way to be sure, but then a suspicion grew in his mind: Had those words 'Ractar Plen' awakened similar memories — simultaneously — in others?

These shadows in his mind seemed to be behind every corner he turned. Fen became so cautious that he would only enter and leave their hideaway using the hidden tunnels. He jury-rigged and placed sensors within a click perimeter of the shed to warn of anyone approaching.

Charin also had become vigilant. In spite of their isolation, there were a few neighbors. The closest was three and a half clicks. Each week Charin dutifully trudged the distance over the bumpy landscape to their neighbor. Wide detours around the many bomb craters often slowed her progress. "Pops" was a crusty old guy who didn't mind telling a pretty girl everything that went on in their extended neighborhood if she would just stay a little longer.

All these precautions had not been enough.

"Sensor six alarm!" Charin yelled from the shed through the hidden door to Fen.

Fen bolted from the inner rooms, closing the hidden door behind him just a moment before a scarlet red Lars smashed through the shed door. Lars' snap-stick was in his belt and his hand rested on the weapon.

"Well! Isn't this cozy," Lars sneered.  "I thought it was strange, your reluctance, to leave this... dump... and come to Capital with me," he spat toward Charin.

"It's not what you think, Lars," Charin said calmly.  "I've hired Fen to haul artifacts from the site for me.  You can check with Labor if you don't believe me."

"Oh, I believe you alright," Lars said, stepping uncomfortably closer to Charin.  Suddenly he struck a cruel blow to her face with the side of his hand, sending her sprawling onto the dusty dirt floor. "Bitch!"

Furious, adrenaline pumping, Fen started to jump at Lars then restrained himself. Lars had drawn his snap-stick and was pointing it straight in Fen's face.

"What I see is a foolish underage girl being beaten and seduced by a violent offender who will go to Chambers," Lars sneered. "And the poor girl, who had been warned of association with such influences, had her permit cancelled and was confined," he predicted. "Of course, I may rescue her from confinement if we immediately marry," he schemed to himself.

What happened next was a blur.

Charin picked herself up from the floor, turning her back toward Lars. Then quickly, with one continuous unexpected motion she forcefully smashed her right heel into Lars' groin. The air around her began to haze and shimmer. Her eyes glazed into a hard black glare, her face wore an insane grimmace, a look Fen had never seen before. "Ahhhgghhh!" screamed Lars in agony as he doubled over still clutching the snap-stick.

Instantly Fen leaped forward at Lars just as Charin yanked the snap-stick from his hand with enormous force. Fen heard the crack as several of Lars' fingers broke as he fell to the floor. Fen stepped back.

Charin was pointing the weapon at Lars but now she turned it directly on Fen. The room itself seemed to wave in a haze. She smiled a cruel smile at Fen. In a deep, scratchy, guttural voice, not her own, she hissed: "Get out of my way!" Fen could see her hand already moving on the trigger mechanism. Without thought, Fen feigned weakness and a fall, then coming up under the snap-stick pushed it upward just as it went off with a loud "braaakkkk!"

The shot went wild, hitting a huge rotten beam in the wood and metal ceiling of the shed. The beam end dropped with a roar of dust and debris smashing Lars skull where he lay writhing doubled-up on the floor. Charin crumpled like a marionette whose strings had been cut.

Lars was dead. Charin lay there, unconscious, hardly breathing. Fen softly and carefully took the weapon from Charin's hand and fell back onto a nearby bench, stunned. What should he do now?

\* \* \*

After what seemed an eternity to Fen but was actually less than a minute, Fen gently lifted Charin's limp body from the floor. Opening the panel to the hidden rooms with his foot, he carried her to the low cot in the corner of the inner room and covered her with a blanket. Making sure she was breathing normally, he ducked back into the shed to examine Lars.

Blood pooled around Lars' smashed head, slightly darker than the scarlet of his new uniform.

Hours later (by the time Fen heard Charin reviving in the innermost room) he had jacked the broken roof beam almost back into position and secured it with a metal post. He carefully searched Lars, removing his uniform, all rank bands and idento. Then he encased the lifeless body into several wide pieces of thermo-sheet (normally used to pack artifacts) and dragged the corpse to the outer of the two hidden rooms. In the shed, he did his best to clean up and erase as many traces of the struggle as he could. As he returned to the inner room, to check on Charin, he looked down at Lars' wrapped-up body and thought, "I didn't really know you, Lars, and although you were always a pain for me, I release you and wish you luck with any deity you may believe in."

He brought Charin some hot jaran tea and sat down on the edge of her cot. She was sitting up now huddled in the blanket shaking. "I don't know what happened," she said gratefully sipping the tea. "Is he...?"

"Dead, yes...," answered Fen. She shuddered. "I've removed everything from him and wrapped him in thermo-sheet," Fen continued, "I don't know what some of the things I found on him are, and when you are stronger I need your help to identify them."

As she put down the tea, memory returned to her. "I... almost killed you! Something happened to me. I'm *so* sorry!" she gasped. Suddenly breaking down, she leaned and grabbed Fen around the neck, sobbing. Fen quietly put his arms around her and said nothing.

# CHAPTER EIGHT

## Discovery

Charin awoke suddenly and looked around. "How long have I been knocked out?" she asked just as Fen came through the main opening from the outer chamber.

"At least five hours," he replied. "We need to talk."

Fen held a small cloth bag in his hand. Carefully he pulled several objects from the bag and lay them on a small shelf next to the cot where she sat.

"I took these from Lars. They were hidden beneath his uniform and I don't know what they are," he said. "I hope you'll recognize them."

Charin picked up a sectioned, hinged bracelet in one hand. It was scarlet and made of a hard non-metallic substance and gave off a luster. Getting up, Charin pushed her hair out of her eyes. Reaching into a box she grabbed a hair tie and pulling her hair back tied it with the other hand. She then walked to her workbench, turned on a mini-light affixed behind a large magnifier and placed the bracelet on the viewing stage to examine it. The bracelet seemed decorative under normal light, but when she tried the ultraviolet range a symbol blazed from one section — two interlocking hooks — it was Kill Corps.

Fen brought the other objects from the shelf over to her workbench for her to examine. The school ring seemed normal enough.

"What's this?" Fen said pointing to a foot-long flat pouch. "I tried to open it, but it doesn't have any opening I can find."

"It's a portodoc," Charin informed him, "if you force it open it gives off an alarm. You need an audio code to open it, but it's not personal voice-keyed. We can override it with a field."

Pulling a generator like a serving plate from a box below her bench, Charin moved a slider on its side and several indicator lamps lit up. Placing the portodoc in the center, she fiddled with two other sliders on its side. She reached a resonance point and stopped adjusting the sliders.

Leaning over the plate, Charin quietly said: "Open." On the portodoc a long slotted pocket was smoothly revealed.

Charin slid two folded documents from the portodoc, opening the first one. Fen looked over her shoulder as she read:

"Kill Corps Appointment

Know that as of this day Lars Penfarud of Clan Greka is duly appointed as junior adjutant to Capital Council Extortion Committee.

Any and all actions he may perform in the line of duty are extra-legal and only answerable to this committee. He is to be released of any liability for persons killed or property destroyed. Any person or authority attempting to waylay or delay him are subject to Chambers. Any person or authority failing to comply to his orders are subject to Chambers.

He has the right of the scarlet band and uniform.

He has the right of transponder.

Frake- Grand Overseer, Kill Corps"


The document was dated slightly after Lars first visit. Wordlessly, Charin moved the first document aside and opened the second and began to read:


"To: Lars Penfarud
From: Frake, Grand Overseer

You did a good job on your first assignment. I don't know why you would want to marry such a lowly slut. But here is my authorization for twenty days. If you must, wed her, bed her, and set her up in Capital. Have your boy Krek live at your place and assign him to watch her and report. If that doesn't slake your appetite, hypno her and set up a mistress or two in the outlying districts.

Report back on time. The Seer knows there's treason afoot and we have work to do."

This document was dated two days ago. Shuddering, Charin dropped the documents back onto the plate. "You bastard!" she said aloud to the air in front of her. She felt the violence of rage surge within her and wanted to rush into the next room to savage Lars' body. This overwhelming emotion was something she had felt only once before – when she had mysteriously attacked Fen. Straining for control, she turned to Fen. She put her hand on his and chokingly muttered, "I need a minute." Fen turned and walked into the outer room while she composed herself.

Fen worried. Angry with himself, he felt the same way he had felt during their first search of the rebel pod – he was missing something. "I've got to trust myself," he thought. "I know what is going on – somehow I remember – I just can't seem to see it clearly." Reflecting on recent events, for the first time he began to distrust Charin. She had turned on him. Turpante had turned on him too. He had blocked Charin's attack, but how had he handled Miss Turpante?

He thought back to that traumatic day in class years ago. He pictured the events in his mind as he had done so many times in the past. He tried to recall every detail of the event. This time, he heard again her fist crash into the wall above his head as he fell, then all went black. With great effort he went over it all again and again. Finally, the blackness at the end lifted somewhat and he heard a voice, like his own, say: "Stand Down." "Was that me?" he puzzled.

There were immediate problems to solve. They *had* to access the full rebel database. "I'm sure a lot of our answers are there," he reasoned, "Without data we're cooked! What can we do with Lars' body? If Lars had a transponder placed in his body when he joined Kill Corps, then it will be activated when he doesn't report — in just seventeen days! It will be traced straight to this shed... they probably won't be interested in talking."

# CHAPTER NINE

## Unlocked

The tension between them was palpable. "NO! Not that!" Charin snapped at Fen as she swatted his hand from the console control. She bit her lower lip. "We're near total exhaustion," she thought, "we can't go on this way much longer."

Reading her mind, Fen said aloud, "We're getting nowhere and we're both near the breaking point." Charin ignored him.

It had been three days and nights since Lars had died and his body still lay in the outer room. Charin had pushed a growing tumult of scattered emotions and shadowy thoughts from her conciousness to continue work. Fen experienced a mounting helplessness as he took to pacing the inner room back and forth aimlessly. Pouring over decrypting the rebel database, they had barely taken time to eat or relieve themselves – all to no avail – and the database remained sealed.

"Charin, Enough!" Fen finally burst out grabbing her wrists from their position on console, "We need to get out of here and talk." Charin was furious but Fen was firm. Pulling her to her feet he gently but forcefully pushed her toward the exit.

It was night outside when they finally emerged. The pale Child Moon shown through the constant haze as they walked distractedly along an ancient street in the ruins. It was light enough that Fen could see remains of doorways in the crumbled foundations that littered the side of their walkway. As they walked their mood seemed to lighten and Charin broke the silence.

"I'm sorry I snapped at you, but I really don't know what else to try. I was never trained to deal with this level of encryption."

"I understand," Fen said. "I can see that you're doing your best and I also want to thank you for teaching me so much. I was forbidden any Tech study for so many years, but now I have funny, fuzzy memories, some are like Tech dreams, some are places, some are... well... almost-remembered names."

"When did that start?" she asked, puzzled.

Not answering, he stopped and motioning to her, they sat on a carved stone bench that a strolling couple might have used six-thousand years before.

"I'm not exactly sure, since I was about nine years old I think," he finally responded. "Maybe if you explain what you need, I could help," Fen asked, changing the subject.

"It's the final key," she explained. "I know part of it, but there's no way other than guessing that I can complete it."

"What *do* you know?"

"I know what the first part is: 'tarpa den' for level two," she said.

'Tarpa den'!? Hearing the words, stunned, Fen reeled as if he had been hit.

"Are you alright?" Charin said as Fen almost fell off the bench.

"I... I'm... very blank. I hear words. Words? They're: 'bar did leptar'," he croaked in a shaky voice.

"What do they mean?" She put her arm around him to hold him upright.

"Keys!" he gasped, voice still shaky.

They sat there over an hour until Fen recovered. "How do you feel now?" Charin finally ventured.

"Alright, but I have a loud ringing in my ears. I think we should go back now. I don't know why... but add the words to your key and I know it will decrypt."

With her arm still around Fen steadying him, Charin somewhat shakily retraced their steps along the dim moonlit path back to the shed and into the hidden inner room.

Sitting again in the glow of the console, Charin keyed the phrase at the proper levels — the database unlocked. Their exhaustion left as they began to examine data that had been hidden for one hundred and twenty-two years.

# CHAPTER TEN

## Dispersing and Disposing

Alarmingly, only thirteen days remained until Lars was due to report back. They had no way of knowing when his hidden transponder might be activated. Fortunately Lars' body was located (for at least the present) where his superiors presumed him to be. Unless life-functions were also monitored, there was still some margin of safety.

"We're exposed here," Fen announced to Charin as they sat eating their sparse protein rations sitting on the bench in the marginal shade of the overhanging metal roof in front of the shed. "Our extra rooms are fine for prying neighbor's eyes, but we are not shielded from a low-level tactical scanner's piercing rays. We need a secure place, and we need it fast!"

"Well, let's get packing, even if we don't really know where we're going!" said Charin patting him on the knee and smiling which broke Fen out of his brooding mood.

Immediately that morning Fen and Charin started gathering and packing all the equipment and devices they had removed from the rebel pod as well as her "research" equipment. They were stacking it in the outer room.

Using make-shift handles she had taped to its side, Charin hefted a large crate just as Fen walked into the outer chamber. "Have you figured out where we are taking all this?" she panted. "There's nothing left in the inner room now except our cots."

"I'm not certain, but I've been thinking," Fen answered. "A Kill Corps officer would *never* take public transport to get here. I figure Lars hid a scooter nearby – probably to impress you."

"Or to drag me back to Capital hypno'd," she thought turning away from him to conceal her wince. "I've had a thin escape from a horrid life as Mrs. Lars Penfarud... however short my life may be now."

Puzzled a bit by her hidden face, Fen frowned, "Anyway, I've been out scouting around to see if I could find the scooter."

Together they searched for Lars' craft. It took an entire day. "My God!" he said when they found it. Fen had envisioned a small scooter. There before him was a fully armed patrol cruiser. The cruiser was equipped for twenty men in battle gear and had limited orbital capability. In his arrogance, Lars had come alone. The cruiser sat there on its struts, a dull black with a scarlet band. One look at that stripe and no one in their right mind would even approach it – no wonder it was not locked.

"We could fly it to the shed and pick up our stuff," Charin advanced, but Fen disagreed.

"If we activate it now, we could start an alert and they would come immediately to investigate," he cautioned.

In the end, they spent two more days and nights carefully hauling the rebel equipment from the shed and stowing it in the cruiser. Returning to their hideaway, they removed all concealing panels and filled the hidden rooms with pot shards and artifacts Charin had collected from the ancient site. The escape tunnels were rigged to look like ventilation ducts. Anyone investigating the site would believe the rooms were hollowed out to aid the research excavation in the hot clime.

With ten days left, what to do with Lars' body was a real problem. The multi-layer thermo-sheet embalming had sealed in the decay, but it would do nothing to stop an activated transponder signal.

Charin reassured Fen, "If we put the body in the cruiser its shielding will keep the transponder from being triggered."

Finally, they distastefully placed the cadaver on a long, wide board and attaching ropes to the board, like a sled, they dragged it toward the cruiser. Neither of them relished carrying around a corpse. After they had painfully hauled the body halfway to the cruiser, Fen realized, "If we take this body with us, every time we open the outside hatches, the transponder might activate."

Hours later they gave Lars a quick funeral. Fen had a bright idea. Pulling the body away from the crusier, they dragged it in the opposite direction and deposited it inside the old crashed rebel pod where its shielding would isolate any potential transponder signal activation. Pausing a moment, feeling strange, Fen apologized to the bones of great-grandfather and his loyal crew for placing a traitor within their midst. He vowed to return and remove the intruder — if he survived. Closing the hatch, they shoveled dirt over it to cover any trace of their presence. The pod had been a tomb already.

# CHAPTER ELEVEN

## Big and Little Fish

There were seven days to go until Lars would be missed. Fen found some paint in the cruiser's utility locker and spent hours painting out the feared scarlet stripe with the hull-matching black drab used by the domestic police. Finishing the job and hauling the remaining supplies into the cruiser, Fen passed Charin. She sat semi-reclined, hair tied-back, legs crossed, propped up on an elbow. Her shapely torso was almost striking an artist's pose on the ship's console. She was studying cruiser operational manuals. She looked lovely, as though perched on an elegant couch, not on the severely functional console amid the military-oriented grey environment. Looking up, she saw a dirty, paint-stained Fen.

"You've been painting all this time?" she said.

"Yes, but at the same time I've been thinking about more important things," was his grim reply. Lightening his mood, Fen added, "Such as what are we going to name this craft I just painted? I think we should christen it 'Luck' — what do you think?" he chuckled, revealing a broad smile.

"I think that's entirely appropriate... we're going to need it!" she laughed easing the tension for a moment.

They took an entire day to rest, plan and prepare. Luck was exactly what they had. The cruiser was equipped with everything twenty men would need on a campaign to win a small war. Weaponry, rations, ammunition, fuel, sophisticated sensors (some of which they had no clue how to use), pressure suits, gear of all kinds was furnished in abundance and carefully stowed. Two heads and a shower were off the crew's barracks. All of their equipment from the shed used only a small portion of the cargo bay and was now carefully tied-down and secured there. A small galley was provided with a drop-down table around which about five people could sit, about the only place on-board one might call "cozy". They realized how lucky they were that the over-confident Lars had not brought "friends" with him.

"You have friends, you know," Charin had counseled Fen late that night as they huddled in the galley over huge mugs of hot tea, "they simply could not reveal themselves... they... they're part of the resistance." She let this sink in, then continued, "I know you would have been part of it also if you hadn't been railroaded into Dog Corps."

Fen, to his surprise, felt his face flush and his body heat up as he suppressed his emotions. At school he had felt *furious* at what he considered their cowardly betrayal. Now for the first time he understood that they were *compelled* to lay low.

Shocked, Fen asked, "*All* of my friends? Which ones?"

"I've broken an oath to tell you this much," she confessed, "but I'll talk with them when we get to Capital. We're going to need help."

That night, despite the overly firm barracks bunk on the cruiser, Fen slept a bit less uneasily.

After some early morning preparations, Charin walked into the nearby town at midday. It was already dark when she returned.

"Well, it's done," Charin declared as she climbed into the Weapons Officer chair in the cruiser. Fen, with his feet propped up on the control console, was sitting in the Pilot's chair next to her immersed in an active tablet on his lap. "I've sent off my 'Ancients of the Loyal Clans' paper with two boxes of supporting pot shards and a vase to Capital School. Mars Bebtar in archeology will think it's fair work. I stole most of it from a fifty-year-old journal. I wonder if that makes me a disrupter?" she quipped. Fen was glad that she still had retained her sense of humor.

"Did you tell them in town that you would be leaving and returning to Capital and did you drop my Labor resignation papers terminating me?" Fen asked.

"Yes, and there were no questions, but the Labor boss said, 'Good riddance'," she added.

"It's time. We better get started," Fen announced.

He quickly folded away the active tablet he had been using and Charin jumped. He observed her nervousness and waited expectantly. "I've... I've never done anything like this before," she blurted out.

"Neither have I, but we have 'Luck' with us," he jibed. They both laughed nervously.

Charin *was* tense. She had never flown anything as large as this cruiser. After the tragic death of her mother in an accident, her father had allowed her to fly scooters and other lite sport craft. She had won some awards in competitions for her age group, but what she was about to attempt was clearly another level. She was a Tech 4 and although theoretically, the technical, mechanical parts of flying the cruiser were not that difficult or different, it did not replace the training and experience a real pilot would have.

They switched chairs. Charin took the Pilot's seat and Fen manned the weapons position. Powering the screens and bringing main power on-line, slowly Charin advanced the power lever to the "hover" detent. A low hum permeated the craft as

Charin retracted the struts. Raising the craft to fifty feet, she steered slowly noticing the craft's slow, heavy response to the controls. Gingerly, she made some slow 'S' turns maintaining her altitude.

"What's up?" asked Fen.

"I need to understand the 'feel' of these controls, they respond way, way slower than the light scooters I'm familar with." Charin responded biting her lower lip and frowning in concentration.

After a few minutes of maneveuring and some slight rolling turns, Charin navigated to a nearby waiting point beneath the calculated flight path of the twice-daily local commercial carrier.

They did not have long to wait.

On schedule, the carrier rose slowly from the town station into the darkening sky. "Here it comes," she said watching a dot on their screen. As it started to rise more quickly it came over the top of them. Charin smoothly shot the cruiser up under it to within five feet of the belly and matched its speed and climb rate. She engaged the auto-follow program she'd created.

In the carrier above, the co-pilot's gauge momentarily reacted. "Ground echo indicated," he casually told the pilot. "Hrummph." the pilot acknowledged chewing a z-bar.

Soon they were cruising along like a little fish attached to the bottom of a big fish. Continental defense would only see one craft (they hoped). "If we get away with this 'big fish' trick, we'll be in Capital in two hours," a slightly more relaxed Charin whispered to Fen as though Kill Corps and the passengers in the carrier above could hear her. "Then the fun begins."

# CHAPTER TWELVE

## A Fright

"We're starting our descent," Charin said softly as she nudged Fen who was fighting sleep at the weapons station. She wanted to let him sleep, but now the most dangerous part of their subterfuge was about to begin and she needed his help.

Fen rubbed his eyes and stretched, "How are we doing?" he queried.

"We've entered the Main Station space at Capital." she responded. "The tricky part," she continued, "is when to break off from hiding. Too high and they'll pick us up on their screens, too low and we could get too close to Main Station and be visually spotted or worse, clip something."

"How long until we break off?" Fen said trying to scan the screens while still rubbing his bloodshot eyes.

"Depends," she answered. "The ideal height comes as we match the domestic traffic lanes. If our 'big fish' carrier comes in toward Capital he'll have to turn just before main artery and I can slip straight into the traffic lane. We'll only be exposed for maybe two minutes. If, on the other hand, he goes into Station away from Capital, I'll have to break out higher and go around to the lane slowly.

It could take ten minutes because I can't go in front of him or else he'd pick us out."

Minutes felt like hours as the craft they were hovering beneath decreased velocity and slowly descended. "He's turning away from Capital," Charin staccatoed to Fen. Their new route was even farther away from the traffic lanes than they had planned. They had no choice but to follow.

Fen now turned on the weapons circuits to prepare for a possible firefight. A sudden hum pulsed in their craft. Both jumped as though they'd been hit. Tearing her eyes from the screens, Charin glared. He nodded back as if to say: "Sorry."

"Getting close to break off." Charin announced checking her seat restraint with a forced calm. Fen saw what she was doing and tightened his own restraint then returned his sweating palms to the weapons controls. He saw her hand reach for the control that would initiate a fall and commit them to a desperate twenty-five minute race to the anonymity of domestic traffic. Her hand froze over the control.

"What's happening?" Fen probed.

"He's stopped descending and is turning and going a new route... toward Capital! It's highly unusual," she said. Had they been discovered?

There was no option but to follow for the time being. For thirty painful minutes 'big fish' flew on, eventually overflying the domestic lanes. Then, in a slow, wide sweeping turn, the carrier headed toward Station resuming its descent. As they were about to pass over the domestic lanes the screen showed almost no traffic at this late, late hour. "Luck" was closer to the lanes than either Charin or Fen ever expected or hoped for.

"Now!" Charin shot her hand to a control. Their patrol craft plummeted onto main artery, their stomachs leaping to their throats. Their bodies slammed into the restraints as Charin abruptly slowed to traffic speed.

"So far so good," Fen mumbled pushing himself back into his seat to loosen the chafing restraints.

Unbelievably they had been uncovered for only ten seconds.

Slowly they wove their way along the uncrowded traffic lanes out of Capital to the suburbs. "Where exactly am I going?" queried Charin as Fen directed their route.

"To a place I sneaked into as a kid with the other boys. We were chased out enough to know there's only one guard and I thought of it the first time we saw this cruiser." Fen responded.

"Great, thanks for the detailed information." Charin quipped.

Fen continued to give Charin directions toward a very low-rent, industrialized section of Capital she had never explored. "We're here!" Fen finally said. Their patrol cruiser hovered at one-hundred feet. On the screen using only the diffused light of a half-full Child Moon they could see dim shapes. Mile-long rows of hulks were lined up in semi-circular array. At the center of the arc, three distant lights on tall poles like bright points pierced the dark attempting to illuminate the dusty road in front of the first row of hulls.

"Can I use scanners? I can't see enough through the screens, the lights interfere," Charin asked Fen as she manipulated the controls, holding their position.

"You can't use scanners or they're sure to set off an alarm. I'm going to open the hatch and visually spot," he replied.

Stepping down onto the deck plate, Fen went to the side hatch. He killed the white internal lights and switched on a deep red night-light glow. Fastening a safety belt around his waist, he secured it to the side of the hatch with a line and opened up. Cold night air washed his face as he gazed down on the sea of wrecked and mothballed cruisers, *each one nearly identical to their stolen cruiser.* There were five rows, here and there a cruiser was missing.  "Something near the center," he thought straining his neck. "I wish we could go higher, then it would be easy."

At last he saw a vacant position in the middle row near one end of the arc.  Through hand signals he directed Charin and they settled in the midst of the junk.  Charin extended the struts then powered off.

They had arrived.

# CHAPTER THIRTEEN

## Worried

Fen and Charin were sitting on a blanket in the shade, the warm breeze slightly fragrant as it stroked his face. Charin was all eager to tell him about mathematics and science. Fen waited, excited to hear her every word. He watched her lovely breasts slowly rising and falling with each breath. All about her face the world appeared blurred.

Fen softly leaned closer to her and placed his hands... on her throat and started to choke her with all his strength. Her eyes glared a dull black with hatred. The space seemed to distort and he was aware of a black bulk behind her. In a deep, scratchy, guttural voice she hissed: "Killer Fen, haaaa, haaaaaaa!" "No! No! Stop!" he screamed to himself all the while convulsively tightening his fingers around her neck.

Fen jolted awake from his nightmare dripping in sweat. Feeling the stuffy blackness around him like a smothering blanket, he thought for a moment he was back in his cell in night pen. Shaking his head to clear it, he saw the dimly blinking red security sensor lights next to where his head had been. "How long has she been gone?" he asked himself as he sat up on the edge of the cruiser bunk still in the dark.

He had not wanted her to go alone. They had unlocked and removed the reconnaisance skyscooter from its locker suspended above the 'ready' area. Outside the cruiser in the dark they had unfolded its spidery suspension and securely bolted the main rod and arms.

"I think you should wait until dawn," Fen had told her, "these things are hard to ride when you can see where you're going, let alone in the dark with no lights or scanners."

"You know I can't do that," Charin had said, "there are less than five days until Lars will be missed and I need to get to my father's within the hour. There's not a moment to lose."

Fen had paced a few moments then worriedly looking at her said, "Well, I'm going with you. There's room enough for two, although this thing looks like a joke."

"No, you're not!" she argued. "We already agreed that here, hidden in this sea of junk, is our base. If I fail, you'll have to carry on somehow by yourself." Feeding power to the scooter and slowly rising, she hovered a second and said, "Besides, you're the one with 'Luck'." Off she flew with a speed that scared him. She didn't look back.

It had now been six and a half hours since she left. Outside the cruiser it would be late morning and the sun would be baking the cruiser's paint. He really hated to be at odds with her, but he couldn't help feeling that there was something wrong, really wrong. His dream tended to confirm it, something about the dream was all too real.

* * *

Even flying slow and low Charin was freezing. She was dressed for a desert clime and the skyscooter's small fairing did little to block the rushing pre-dawn air. "Maybe, I'm not as smart as I think," she thought as she grimaced against the cold wind. "Easy girl, if your hands get too numb you'll loose control of this thing."

She decided on caution and set the scooter down on a low unpopulated ridge. After she had powered to standby she was suddenly tossed off bruising her knee badly when she hit the ground. One spindly strut of the scooter had slid off the loose rock on which it had landed. It took a good half-hour to rub life back into her numb fingers and to massage her injured knee before trudging back onto the scooter and again shooting skywards. Completing another freezing run, with her hands shaking on the controls, she landed at her father's. She pulled behind a shed and slid under a lean-to far from the main house just as the faintest hint of dawn crept into the night sky.

Charin limped across the back yard toward the guesthouse. She remained just outside the main house security field. Main house Sentry lights indicated that her father was out-of-town.

As soon as Charin saw the guesthouse, a flood of memories engulfed her. After after her mother had died, that was where she had moved. The main house was too full of her mother's missing presence for her to endure. Charin's father had understood her grief and need for solitude and allowed it, although she was only twelve at the time. Here she had privately grieved. Here she had been left alone. Here she had become self-reliant.

"12-Charamine — no lights," she quietly said into the guesthouse's Sentry security pad ('Charamine' had been her mother's private pet name for her in happier times). The indicators on the pad turned off and the guesthouse door gaped opened before her like a black mouth. She stumbled in. "Security level six," she told the house which acknowledged with a low double beep after the door silently slid shut behind her. She was home, she was safe... for now.

"Night blinds, lighting level three," she told the house which complied. She went straight to the bathroom where she was confronted by full-length mirrors that showed a bedraggled girl with stained clothes, tied-back hair, smudged face and a bruised and bleeding knee. "Is this what Fen and Lars and the townspeople saw?" she said, unable to restrain herself, "My God!"

In spite of her longing for a long, hot tub, she quickly showered and changed and feeling much refreshed, sat in a comfortable, white robe eating a fortified protein mix the consistency of pudding, pondering her next steps.

It had now been six and a half hours since she left. Outside the guesthouse it would be late morning and the sun would be high in the sky. She really hated to be at odds with Fen. She had been abrupt with him when she departed. A feeling had been building within her for hours like a dream gone bad. She couldn't help feeling that there was something wrong, really wrong.

# CHAPTER FOURTEEN

## Conspiracy

The backroom at Emzee's Lounge was secure. Piling into the small, noisy chamber with the others, Preed slowly turned on recorded sounds of singing and loud conversation, raising the volume level to match their actual voices as they simultaneously quieted down until the masking was complete. Then, doing a quick buzz scan and finding no surveillance devices, he stuck an operating detector on the wall above the door, nodded to Thara and sat down without a word (blocking the entry door).

Charin sat on the far side sipping a hot drink. Charin looked them over, trying to relax a bit — she knew they all felt awkward, finding themselves together at the same time after such a long time. On top of that, she was sure they would not like what she had to say.

Preed grimly eyed her from across the room. They had dated last year and she knew he wanted her. He was older and they had not hit it off. His stolid, serious demeanor had put her off any romantic interest, yet they remained close friends and his trustworthiness was beyond question.

Lall and Nar were like inseparable twins. They had grown up together since young boys.

Athletic and solidly built, honest not bright. Despite the severity of the situation, they were playing the adolescent game of teasing Gem.

Gem, a brilliant but sensitive Tech One, was an unfocused dreamer. Charin knew he could have helped her solve the database dilemma days earlier had he been available. Once focused, Gem was formidable.

And last there was Thara with her long, red hair which seemed to flash whenever she turned her head. Her temperament was as fiery as her hair. She was not one to cross, yet Charin probably would likely have a run-in with Thara when she said what she must. She had used one of the "three secret ways" in order to get them all here. It was ironic that until now they probably did not even know that each of them were part of the underground order.

Thara turned to Charin, "Before we start, just tell me one thing... are you really going to marry that pig Lars?"

Charin bit her lip. "I will not be marrying him, Thara ...period." Charin took a deep breath and started to begin.

"Don't be so sure," Thara interrupted rudely, "he's been blackmailing your father and boasting of your upcoming elopement all over. How are you going to get out of it?  He now wears the red uniform."

"The sign has been given, let her speak," Preed interjected, slightly annoyed.

Standing in the corner, Charin felt (not a little) trapped. "Over a year ago, Fen Dathrod and I made an archival discovery here in Capital." Charin chokingly began. "It not only proved Fen's innocence but led to other documents.  This resulted in my leaving Capital to do my final school year at a remote archeological site.  Ancient archeology was not the reason I went.  I went to meet up with Fen and search for a fantastic relic of the rebellion."

She really had their attention now as they huddled closer to hear her over the loud voices of the masking disc playing near the door.  Her feeling of being closed in increased and sweat poured down her neck.  Preed did not leave his seat but continued blocking the door while straining to hear her.

"We found the relic... and I have shocking news.  Everything we thought we knew about the rebellion is in the majority false.  The truth is, we are facing a major disaster for everyone on Dactoes if things continue in their course."

She paused a bit to let this sink in a bit. Seeing the dazed look on their puzzled faces, "I have proof!" she blurted. Hurriedly continuing (lest she lose her nerve) "...and I have to confess to you that I've taken Fen into my confidence and told him of the existence of our organization."

Thara instantly jumped in her face, "You what! You've broken your oath. You've revealed us all!" Thara had her hands on Charin's collar and was shaking her when Nar and Lall pulled Thara off at Preed's signal.

"Let her cool down," counseled Preed as he helped Charin sit.

Charin noticed Gem was uncomfortably guarding the door in Preed's place. Thara glared, but was for the moment silent. The others sat and stared at Charin with varying degrees of concern, confusion and dismay.

It took an uncomfortable second to recover from Thara's accusation, but with new strength Charin realized she'd have to make a speech. Calling on all her reserves to formulate what to say, she stood.

"I *never* revealed your names. I only said that some of Fen's friends were *really* his friends and I convinced him to let me come here and contact you alone. He and I are playing a deadly game and I don't think we have very good odds for coming out alive. We *need* your help. Dactoes *needs* your help. *You* need to decide whether you are 'in' or 'out' right now. I don't ask this lightly. This is a sacred answer. All our lives, all our families' lives and all the lives of those yet to come depend upon it. I'm not kidding and this is no jest." She sat down.

"We need to consult our group leader. The underground should be informed", Gem pleaded from across the room.

"No!" commanded Preed, "I have something to say."

He slowly stood, his large frame and broad shoulders seeming to fill all the remaining space in the room, his jaw firmly set.

"I *am* your group leader," he confessed. "The time for secrets between us is over. Is there anyone who does not plan to accept Charin's oath?" Silence reigned. "Alright. In fact, I recruited all of you to our (pathetic) rebellion in order to keep that true spirit alive. I know the leaders of the main so-called rebel organization but I suspected they were ineffective, infiltrated and paid to be that way from the start. They know nothing of *this* group of 'rebels' at all. You are the heirs of the actual rebellion, maybe more than you know. Now, swear on your life and any deities you represent that you will help Fen and Charin... I so swear," he began.

One by one they swore the oath.  "Good!" Preed grimly smiled, "Because if any of you hadn't, I would have made sure you would have died in your sleep tonight.  There's more.  Okay Charin tell us what you can, and what we can do to help."

Charin's spirits felt lifted as she heard them swear.  A welling of emotion had come to her eyes and tears of relief rolled down her cheeks. "Thanks," she said, "I thought we were alone."

# CHAPTER FIFTEEN

## No Message Possible

Charin huddled on the soft couch hugging a large pillow. Even though surrounded by the familiar comforting warmth of the guesthouse she had lived in for the last six years, it was hard for her to see any hope for her future. The revelations and events of the preceding couple of weeks had left her frightened. "I hope it doesn't show," she thought hugging the pillow tighter. "Fen and the others are counting on me to be strong."

Finally, she reluctantly rose from the couch and went back to the small travel case open on her bed. Gazing inside she mentally went over the list of things which she thought practical that she had stashed inside. Satisfied, she zipped the case close, lifted it and set it by the door in preparation to leave. Oh how she wished her mother were here to talk to, "Why did she have to fall down the stairs and leave us alone," she sighed wiping her eyes with the back of her hand, "and what about Dad?"

Charin's father was a strong, resolute and dynamic man, sometimes acerbic with others but always kind and respectful of her — even as a very small child. His business travels often made him absent for months at a time, yet he always took time to communicate his itinerary to her in advance. Could it be because she'd been away he had not left word for her?

Wondering if she would ever be back to the guesthouse again, Charin gathered her resolve, took a quick look around and left.

Outside, the night air was pitch black. Charin used a hand to guide herself around the guesthouse walls so she wouldn't trip and sat her case next to the skyscooter behind the shed.

"I've got to get going, Fen will be waiting," she thought to herself. "If we fail, it may be the last time I see Dad and I owe it to him to see him."

Strictly speaking, she should have left hours ago. She had completed her mission but there had been no way she could communicate safely with Fen and they had agreed to her return tonight. She still had to uncover the skyscooter and make the dangerous run back to the boneyard. She shivered involuntarily recalling her former night ride.

Creeping down the walkway that ran toward her father's house, she stood for several minutes concealed in the dark. "Where can Dad be?" She thought. Usually, when he was out-of-town on business the house would be on Security Level Four, yet here was the sentry blinking Level One. "He should be home by now."

At last she felt she could wait no longer. It was only two days now until Lars would be missed.

"I'm going to leave Dad a note," she decided walking to the security sentry post. Giving her dad's code and a "no lights" conditioning, the sentry opened the front door of the main house and she walked in.

Lights instantly blazed as the door slid shut behind her.

"Well! Well! Well! Who do we have sneaking in at this hour?" sneered a red uniformed Krek standing up as two uniformed gooneys grabbed her from behind seizing both her arms. "Lars thought you might pull a trick like this," he chuckled.

"Call off your gooneys, Krek, you have no right to be here or handle me this way," Charin protested.

"This uniform gives me any right I need. I work for Lars now... Mrs. Penfarud"

"That is not my name, nor will it ever be!" Charin fumed.

"Always lovely, even when angry," Krek minced. "You know, I haven't heard from Lars since he went to get you. At first, I figured you and he were off together, but then this last week still not hearing from him, I realized you were probably leading him on a merry chase all over province. Lars is not nice when upset, especially about 'love.'

So I figured his 'true love' just might hightail it to dear old dad's to hide out. We've been sitting here in the dark every night for the last three nights waiting and my men have been losing patience, but not me... and, here you are!"

"How did you get in here? Where is my father?" Charin charged.

"Your dad? I detained him on suspicion of treason in Lar's name. I'm having him held pending the successful marriage of his only daughter to my boss," Krek gibed.

"And what will happen if I refuse?" Charin asked.

"If your father refuses to 'play along' he will probably be tortured then executed, all his property confiscated, and you, my dear," Krek sneered, "...will be confined, or worse."

"But it's not true, my father may oppose some of Council's policies, but he is no traitor! You're playing a *very* dangerous game, Krek." Charin said with fire in her eyes.

"Doesn't matter. I intend to make Master Group Leader this year, and you," Krek smiled greedily, "...are how I'm going to do it."

Krek's goonies smirked and chuckled but did not loosen their grip on her arms. Charin could think of nothing to say. She was sure Fen would come looking for her when she was overdue and be ensnared. "What should I do? How can I get a message to him?" she thought.

# CHAPTER SIXTEEN

## Seek and Hide

"We should know something soon," Preed told Fen from the cruiser's control chair as he watched Fen pace panther-like back and forth on the deck plates. It had almost been a day since Charin was due back and Fen's departure to search for her had only been restrained by reason thanks to the nocturnal arrival of Preed and Gem. Fen was persona non grata in Capital and needed to remain hidden. Preed had put a scrambled message on Thara's public communicator dropbox via a skip switch and asked her to check it out.

Suddenly there was a "beep beep beep" and a blue light on the comm panel flashed. Trace said it was a public callbox with Thara's code. Preed scrambled and put it on speaker so they all could hear.

"Secure?" Thara asked.

"Secure." Preed replied.

"I've been to her house," Thara began, "and there's no one there. It's really odd though, both her guesthouse apartment and the main house look deserted and security's off. I don't like it."

"What about the scooter?" Fen interjected into the comm mic.

"The scooter is still hidden in back. There's a travel case next to it and the scooter itself looks like it hasn't been touched," Thara responded.

"Thanks," Preed said into the comm mic, "Why don't you go hang out at Emzee's and see if you can pick up anything? Check back in about two hours."

"Alright, later." Thara disconnected.

Emzee's Lounge had been Upper's second home throughout their school days. It had been the only place that offered some relief from their colorless, oppressive student life. It had been so for decades of students. Its vast size and diversity of distractions also attracted the off-duty domestic police and group officers which made it the ideal place to hear gossip of all kinds.

Fen stopped pacing and looked Preed in the eye, "Well, at least Charin hasn't crashed on the skyscooter."

They both glanced at Gem. He was sitting at navigation pouring over tech manuals for hours as Charin had done, oblivious to all that was happening around him. He had never imagined he would have to learn to pilot a patrol cruiser in a day. They had planned that Charin would pilot and Gem would be a back up, but with Charin missing, Gem was all they had.

Fen was worried, but tried not to show it. "Well, it will all soon be over one way or another," Fen thought. A hardened determinism swelled within him. He seemed to draw power from a deep, unseen internal source as though he was in a familiar setting. He relaxed. Finally, he laughed and spoke aloud frightening Preed and Gem, "Seven people, with one missing and one day to save a planet before Lars is missed. Let's get to work!"

* * *

Although Capital's Temple Complex was dominated by an impressive High Dome, few knew that deep inside the dome was an inner sanctum... and fewer still had ever been inside.

But Frake had penetrated the inner sanctum to eavesdrop. For rooted in the dome's circular pit, there sat the ancient gray Seer, swaying in his trance, uttering nonsensical babbling and an occasional cryptic prophecy in a hypnotic monotone as old as time.

"There is... a change," the ancient tonelessly uttered as Frake was jolted from his usual routine. "One has awakened who will challenge," the Seer continued.

"What! Where?" Frake demanded. This had not happened in twelve years and then only briefly.

"Close... On the doorstep.  The foundations tremble," the usually undecypherable Seer emotionlessly pronounced.

Frake instantly decided to have that eager fool Lars set up a full security alert when he returned tomorrow.  "Damn! Using humans is such a waste!" Frake swore as he impatiently stormed out of the Temple's inner chamber to leave a personal, not electronic, message for Lars.  No use tipping off anyone who might tap in.

Frake never left the inner chamber, even for months at a time so as always to hear the Seer and to be stationed at the sole Planetary Control console, the hub of his security network.  The unlubricated door slid noisily shut behind him as he stomped out.

"Too late...," the Seer intoned to no one.

* * *

Gem's hands nervously worked the cruiser's controls.  Fen was amazed at how well Gem was doing and tried to look reassuring as Preed's concerned glances at Gem tended to make Gem even more nervous.  "I hope we don't get into a fight," Fen thought.

Fen sat up straight, wearing Lars' scarlet uniform and feeling strange.  Lars' helmet nested under his right arm. It would hide his face and unless Fen met someone who personally knew Lars he might just get away with impersonating him.

Gem sat the cruiser down (with a bone-jarring bump) about a click from Temple. A cruiser would *never* come closer so Fen would have to bluff his way through.

"Are you ready?" Preed asked.

"Yes, wait here for another quarter hour then follow," Fen told Preed, stepping from the cruiser and walking briskly away, in as military a manner he could muster, hoping he resembled Lars' canter.

Fen passed increasing crowds of people none of whom noticed him in the slightest (except perhaps to involuntarily give a wide berth to his dangerous red uniform). As he got two-thirds of the way to Temple on the Council side of the structure, a wave of emotion passed through him. He hit a toe on a slightly uneven part of the pavement and almost stumbled and fell. It seemed very, very familiar. He paused (something he really didn't want to do) and tried to orient himself. A mist seemed to surround him and the busy morning concourse faded. It was evening. He heard voices talking to him. He saw himself reflected in one of the kiosks that had been forbidden here for over a hundred years.

He was shocked, his great-grandfather Fen stared back at him through the reflection. Fen tried to move but was frozen.

Suddenly a sense of foreboding flooded over Fen as the scene shifted. It was now early morning. The kiosks stood like sentinels with long shadows, the concourse was abandoned. It was cold and he was alone. Beside him yawned an open hole in the shape of a hexagon that matched part of the geometric design within the pavement pattern. He was next to a short wall with vertical grooves that ran along the concourse for as far as he could see. Every hundred yards a marker was engraved into one of the grooves and there was one next to the hole. It read: "66". Fen reeled. Another wave of disturbing feelings, hot and cold ran through him.

The mist surrounding him cleared. He was on his knees and suddenly it was crowded mid-morning again. Fen was staring at four feet and the holsters of two weapons.

"How may Domestic assist Corps, Sir?" one of the cops said formally with a tinge of scarcasm, "Are you ill?"

As Fen started to stand, he noticed a groove on the short wall. It read: "66". Instantly he made a decision. "Thank you for your... concern Officer...", Fen read his badge, "...Lug. Yes, I can use both your assistance."

"Come with me," Fen commanded, mimicking Lug's tone. He stomped off at a fast pace back toward the cruiser. "I have a cruiser waiting ahead. You will clear the way for me," Fen ordered as he looked back at them.

"Yes Sir!" Officer Lug responded as he and his compatriot hurried ahead to clear his path through the thick crowd.

To Fen's relief, when they got close enough, the cruiser was still parked where it had been, but there were many other vehicles now starting to arrive. Fen steered the cops toward his cruiser. Through its open door he could see Preed wide-eyed at their approach.

"Halt!" Fen ordered and the cops did so at attention. "You are relieved", Fen said as he arrogantly brushed right past them and into the cruiser slamming the door shut in their faces. The cruiser took off.

"Kill Corps," Officer Lug said with knowing contempt to his companion who nodded his agreement.

* * *

Trying to stay upright Fen swayed drunkenly as he sat down in the cruiser. They slowly escaped

Central caught in the morning traffic surge. Preed looked at Fen, very worried himself.

What was wrong? Fen couldn't focus well. He was hot, dizzy and close to fainting.

* * *

It had been Fen's intention to bluff or bluster his way into minister Jaytee's office. He was the only Council minister who consistently opposed the grip and rule that the Seer imposed upon the Council and therefore upon the planet.

Fen was beginning to piece together what he had learned from the rebel database with the flashes of his own memory originating he knew not where. Somehow he *knew* that he had to be at the right place at the right time tomorrow when Lars was due to report.

It *had* to be today. He would have to waste valuable hours until evening. He would use the ancient entry. He would have to hold himself together. He would go in alone.

A harrased Gem said, "Where to?" his fingers flying over the flight console avoiding traffic.

"Take us to Lars' home," Fen hoarsely told Gem.

"You're kidding?" Preed said.

"No. We need to change the plan. I've got new information and we need a place to hide until dark. Lars' home is actually where this cruiser is expected. We may have to disable any staff he may have, but even with his new position I'm sure he hasn't had time to hire too many gooneys," Fen explained. He wondered where Charin was.

Preed frowned then silently went back to the weapons store and returned shortly with three loaded stun sticks.

* * *

"I want to speak to Mrs. Penfarud," Thara said into the security sentry post at Lars' house.

"Who's calling?" a gruff male voice answered.

"Her friend Thara," Thara replied into the post.

After a long pause, a voice Thara clearly recognized as Krek answered: "She's busy, come back later."

"You can't put me off like that, Krek. I know she's back and I want to see her and hear all the details of the elopement. Charin's the talk of our club, snaring that guy," She lied knowing she had correctly guessed where Charin was.

Upstairs, Krek turned to Charin, "Not one word, or your Dad dies." Charin nodded.

"I'll send someone for you, you can come up," Krek said into his call box.

Downstairs, one of Krek's gooneys led Thara up to the rooftop terrace where she saw Charin lounging in a chair with Krek sitting across from her and a second gooney guarding the door, weapon in hand. The place was much nicer than Thara expected. She suspected Lars had just moved in as there were many unopened boxes in most of the rooms she passed on her way up to a sweeping terrace.

"Charin! Charin! Oh you lucky girl!" Thara exclaimed as she ran to give her a big hug.

"It's good to see you, Thara," Charin said as she stiffly hugged her, "very good."

"I'm expecting Lars at any time and you'll have to leave if he arrives," Krek told Thara.

"That's fine," Thara replied, knowing that with Lars dead that was not very likely to happen.

"How ARE you?" Thara asked raising her eyebrow with a secondary meaning.

"As well as can be expected," Charin said, her eyes boring a hole into Krek across from her.

Thara decided to see if she could get Krek talking. He might foolishly reveal more than Charin was obviously allowed to say in his presence.

"Oh Krek, has Lars thoughtfully had you looking after her?  What with all the excitement... you didn't bother her through the wedding trip did you?  If you did, I want all the details.  Charin will only give me facts," Thara pried.

Krek smiled. "Oh, they've had quite a trip I'm sure, but I wasn't along for the adventure.  I'm sure Lars will have a lot to say when he gets home," he smirked.

"Are you expected to handle this large house just yourself?" Thara shot at Charin.

Before she could answer, Krek said, "Oh no, Lars has a large staff ready to start day after tomorrow, to wait on her every beck and call." Then he added for Charin's benefit, "...And protection, two of her very own bodyguards to safeguard and protect her from harm whenever she goes out!"

"My leash," Charin thought as she glared back at Krek.

"Honey, is there anything you could use?" Thara said directly to Charin.

"Yes," said Charin eyes sparkling, "I could use some 'Luck'!"

As if in answer to that prayer, a patrol cruiser suddenly swooped over them and prepared to decend onto the landing stage at the far side of the terrace.

"Here is Lars now," Krek gloated.

"Got to go!" Thara said walking toward the door to downstairs, "I can find my way out, call me when you are settled." Thara rushed through the door and the gooney forgot to follow awaiting Krek's orders. Thara immediately secreted herself behind some boxes on the floor below the terrace. "What the hell?" she thought.

* * *

"There are people near the landing stage," Gem announced staring into the small screen in front of him he used to pilot the patrol cruiser.

"Put it on the large screens," Fen asked as he stifled another wave of dizziness. Gem fumbled for the correct control. Finding it, the large screens flickered to life and there below him were Krek, Thara and Charin. As he watched, Thara hurriedly walked away toward a door guarded by two armed gooneys and disappeared through it.

Fen jumped up, staggering, motioning to Preed and grabbing a stun stick. Preed belted a snap-stick around his waist (just in case) and together they made their way across the slightly unstable deck to the hatch. Gem's piloting was improving rapidly, but he still needed practice.

"When Gem lands, don't open the door, let them approach. I'll take out Krek and you handle the gooneys." Fen said, "I hope there aren't others."

Preed nodded just as Gem extended the struts and bumped down.

Krek was eager to see Lars. He knew Lars would be furious at not finding Charin. He could hardly wait to bask in the glory that would be his when Lars saw that he Krek had found her and brought her to him. Krek was so preoccupied that he didn't notice the lack of the famous red stripe on the cruiser or its wobbly landing. He took one of his gooneys and paraded to the cruiser's hatch and stood to attention. The second gooney continued to guard Charin's escape.

The cruiser hatch popped open. There stood Fen Dathrod in Lars' uniform. Krek had only a moment to register his surprise until Fen's fist connected with his jaw and he fell to the ground unconscious.

Preed's blast from the stun stick disabled the nearby gooney. The other, seeing what had occurred, fired his snap-stick. Fen and Preed hit the ground. The gooney disappeared into the house.

"After him," Fen yelled.

Preed jumped to his feet running. Just then, the door opened and out fell the second gooney, unconscious, followed by Thara who was smiling. "Too easy," she said.

Gem, Preed and Thara started to remove weapons and tie up Krek and the gooneys.

Fen staggered to a nearby chair. Very relieved to see him, Charin ran to Fen. "Heard you needed some 'Luck'," he quipped, hugging her with a smile... then promptly fainted.

# CHAPTER SEVENTEEN
## Without A Clue

They were worried, very worried. Fen lay unconscious, sweating and shuddering on a small daybed in a staff bedroom. One wall was lined with boxes and as Charin knelt over Fen mopping a cold washcloth across his forehead, the others sat or leaned on the boxes, exhausted and perplexed.

"I don't know what happened," said Preed, "he left the cruiser in fine shape, then suddenly he returned trailing two cops, hopped back in looking drawn and flushed and ordered us here."

Darkness closed in as evening deepened. No one spoke. Finally, Thara hit the wall with her hand startling the others and said, "We *can't* just sit here doing nothing! Lars is due to report in the morning and we don't have a plan. Fen knows something, but we don't even know what's wrong with him! What are we to do?" Charin neatly laid the wet washcloth across Fen's brow, stood and started to speak.

All of a sudden everyone jumped, falling off their boxes or stumbling into the walls! A terrible ringing, wailing, piercing kind of "beep" seemed to come from Fen's prone, quivering body. Preed recovered first and bending over raised Fen's left wrist. There, Lar's "Kill Corps" bracelet was glowing and emitting the nerve-shattering shriek.

Preed touched the center of the now visible corps logo and the sound stopped. He was about to speak to the others when out of the bracelet a voice called, a deep, resonant, evil-sounding, other-worldly voice: "Lars you piece of work, I hope to hell you've finished with that little piece of tail, I have work for YOU to do!"

Preed recovered speedily and hoarsely croaked in a voice he hoped sounded like Lars, "She... she led me on a chase, I'm worn out."

"You sound like shit..." the voice answered, "but you better get it together for tomorrow. Listen, here's what I want you to do... you secure at your end?"

"Yeah," Preed croaked.

"So tomorrow you run down Fen Dathrod – I know you know him, he was one of your most violent sleebs. I hear he can be pleasant right before ripping you to shreds – just my kind of tool. You track him down, I don't care if it takes a week. Find him and recruit him... now wait! I know you hate him, but I have a suicide mission for him, he'll never return. If he cannot be swayed, you have my F6B authorization to terminate him. Understood?"

"Yessir," Preed answered.

"Out" came from the bracelet which stopped glowing and went dead.

Preed, now dripping sweat, quietly slid the "Kill Corps" bracelet off Fen. Wrapping it in Fen's washcloth he walked to a side closet and deposited it into a drawer, closed the drawer and the closet door and returned.

They all stood still, stunned, their skin rigid, stretched tight with a near-death tension.

A *"Personal Communicator,"* my god. Such devices were banned after the revolution under penalty of death. They had lived their entire lives in that shadow and naively never even considered such things still existed. It sunk in, they were temporarily reprieved, "Lars finding Fen" might take longer than a week... but if *that* bracelet voice was the mysterious Frake, what were they actually up against?

* * *

Fen was living a dream. He went places. He saw people. They seemed to like and respect him. He saw his hands, they looked like his hands only a bit different... and then there was the ring. It was a large ring and he seemed to talk into it and it talked to him... funny thing for a ring to do?

There were stars, millions and millions of stars! A black sky with stars. Fen had seen only five or ten stars in his entire life and that was only at the edge of dawn. They had appeared as bright dots through the haze on the horizon just below wave cloud. Why could he now see stars?

Flash, flash, flash. He lazily watched another big, black bean rise up from the ground through the haze, higher and higher, then there were flashes, then the bean would slowly fall, but two or more others would rise to take its place. Flashes, then two fell and fifteen others rose. He felt very, very sad watching them. Very odd.

* * *

Late the next afternoon, Charin, Preed, Thara and Gem held a war-council in the small staff bedroom. Lall and Nar joined them. The warm, rounded cream-colored room, with its soft cove lights seemed to fulfill their need for closeness in the otherwise cold, cavernous box-filled rooms of the estate. Fen still lay there on the daybed unconscious, but was breathing easier and had stopped sweating. An entire day had passed and although worried, they all were in better shape for having rested.

Always practical, Preed began logically, "Well, I think we should start by reviewing the facts of our situation as we see them, then we can propose how to proceed." The others nodded agreement and Preed continued, "Fen has become our leader. He and Charin uncovered the data that Dactoes itself is under threat. With this news we have become the *only* people who can do something to stop it and have sworn to do so."

"Unfortunately, Fen did not share all of his plans with us before he dropped into this fitfull sleep, so we'll just have to try to figure out what he had in mind and hope he recovers and soon."

"I think Charin knows the most, so I suggest we let her tell us what she will."

Charin rose, thoughtfully biting her lip and with a nod to Preed began.

"Well, Preed's right, I do know a bit — but not enough. I think I know Fen well enough to say that I believe he was planning some heroic, all alone, tactic that would get *us* off-the-hook." Charin brushed a tear from her eye and continued,

"What we do know is this. Fen and I found an abandoned, wrecked rebel pod and recoved an active console. We decrypted the data log and found out that there is a thousand-year plan to enslave and eliminate all life... *our* life on the planet. We know the name of the plan."

Preed interjected, "Fen told me (on the way to Temple Dome) what his plan was: Dressed as Lars, Fen would bluff his way into Council Minister Jaytee's office. Then he'd privately reveal the thousand-year plan to him and ask his help. It was all he could come up with based upon the time we had before Lars was to report."

Thara jolted upright, a strange gleam in her eye. "Foolish," she cried. "What's the name of the plan?"

"I don't want to speak it out loud," said Charin, "I have a theory I want to test."

Bending to Thara's ear, Charin whispered: "Rachtar Plen."

Thara stood back with a glazed look, the air around her seemed to start to shimmer. The room itself seemed to wave in a haze. Thara smiled a cruel smile. In a deep, scratchy, guttural voice, oddly similar to the one of the bracelet, she hissed: "Get out of my way!" and with a snarl she leaped on Charin clutching her fingers around Charin's throat as she slammed her into the wall.

Charin seemed to have expected something like this so Thara's initial attack was not as lethal as it might have been. Completely amazed, Preed and Lall dragged Thara away from Charin, surprised at Thara's great strength. Suddenly,

Thara collapsed on the floor in a heap as though flipping off a switch.

"Well, now we're getting somewhere!" said Charin smiling wryly and rubbing her throat.

Thara stirred groggily on the floor, Lall opened a nearby box labeled "pillows" and pulling a large decorative pillow from it put it carefully under her head. "What happened?" she asked looking up dazed, then with a horror of returning memory, "My god! I attacked Charin!"

"Please, tell us *exactly* what you remember happening..." asked Charin gently pushing Thara back onto the pillow as she shakily tried to rise.

"Well... I'm not completely sure," Thara started haltingly. "I felt funny when you started talking about 'The Plan,' then you said something into my ear and my head started buzzing. I didn't feel like myself. Come to think of it, I didn't feel at all! Just numb. I was moving... like in a dream. Next thing I knew I was lying here... and let me tell you, my head aches terribly and I'm sore all over!"

"Just rest for now," Charin said, "I want to tell you all what happened the day Lars died."

She had every bit of their attention now. Suddenly they became aware of how dark it had become in the little bedroom. "Lights. Level 2," muttered Preed and the soft glow emanating from a cove around the edge of the ceiling intensified.

"The same thing that just happened to Thara happened to me," Charin continued. "Fen and I had just found out about 'The Plan' and we heard its name. Then Lars burst into the room with a snap-stick. Lars hit me and I decked him with a kick and took the stick. Then the buzzing started in my head, next thing I knew I was starting to shoot Fen...."

Several of the others in the room gasped,

"The stick went off and Fen dodged. The wild shot hit the roof and the roof caved in. A beam collapsed on top of Lars and killed him! When I came to, Fen had carried me to a cot and I felt just like Thara does now."

No one spoke.

"I felt so foolish. I didn't want to talk to anyone about it. I thought there was something wrong with ME! Just tonight I realized that might not be the case, so I made a test... sorry Thara, but it was important. There is something dangerous occurring on the planet that affects us *all* directly. We need to find out *exactly* what it is so we can plan what to do next."

"Can you somehow manage to buy me at least a couple days of research time?" she implored. "And I'll need Gem's help as well. I also think what is going on with Fen is also tied to the same problem. We need him badly," she said. Turning her back to them and looking down at the sleeping Fen she intoned quietly, "I need him badly!"

\* \* \*

They bought Charin more than a couple days. Several pressing problems had been solved.

Krek and the two goonies had been stripped and tied up on the floor of a basement chamber in Lars' estate. Thara enjoyed holding a snap-stick on Krek and crew as they took turns guarding their prisoners. Krek, virtually foaming, showered Thara with insults and curses whenever it was her turn to watch them. One of the prisoner goonies actually begged Thara to tape Krek's mouth shut as they were sick of hearing his whining and sputtering.

"Can't do that," Thara told the goonie.

"Why not?" asked the goonie.

"Because," she snickered, "...he leaks information."

Using information obtained from Krek, Thara posed as Mrs. Penfarud's assistant and postponed the arrival of the new staff Lars had summoned, feigning "incomplete construction" on "house repairs".

The two additional goonies that Krek had ordered to be "bodyguards" for Charin (on Lars' behalf) were more difficult to handle. Having two more prisoners on their hands was going to be troublesome — or worse, a firefight might break out if they tried to subdue them.

A nervous Preed, dressed tightly in Krek's undersized uniform, met the new goonies, snap-stick in hand, "guarding" the main door to the house. Thara, Lall and Nar — hidden just inside and also armed — backed up his position.

"Halt," Preed commanded, gesturing with his stick.

"What's the deal?" asked one of the surprised goonies with a smirk.

"Here's the deal," Preed quipped, "Lars likes his bitches hot, so no "H" for her." he said mimicing a Hypno-helmet being put on.  "We've prepared a 'special' room for her... if you know what I mean (wink)... and she's in it!  We won't need the extra precautions, so you're off the case, order of Krek."

They all held their breath... would the goonies buy it?

"Shit! Poor bitch, wonder how long she'll last?" said one goonie in mock concern. "Tell Krek he better have another one Lars likes ready when this one's used," said the other goonie as they turned about and walked briskly away smiling.

* * *

It was a funny, fuzzy day. Fen lay propped up on a pillow being fussed over by a person with cherubic face on a head too little for his athletic body. Although his vision was hazy, Fen recognized it was Nar. He tried to speak, but the sound that came from his lips was just a croak. Nar smiled, nodded and motioned for him not to try to speak. The drink of water in his dry mouth followed by the soup Nar baby-fed him started to help him recover more.

Fen formed the word "When?" with his lips, "Not now, later, just rest, you have time." Nar answered the unspoken request. Nar's words went through his head, each like a sharp pin causing him to grimace.

How could this be? Lars was due to report. They would be arrested and sent to "Chambers." He had to protect the others. He had to defeat "The Plan" or die trying....

Nar disappeared from the room and Fen tried to stand but he could barely control his body.

His hands were useless, but he could turn his head now and with great effort move his legs. He swung his legs on the daybed to sit up and a wave of dizziness swept over him. Just then Nar returned, bringing Charin and Gem with him.

Seeing Fen awake, Charin smiled, but she looked drawn and unkempt, as though she had not slept in days.

"Fen! Are you alright? I've... 'er, we've been worried." Charin blurted.

Fen was able to nod slightly and, feeling stronger, with great effort muttered, "Dreams..."

"I know," said Charin grimly, "Gem and I have been working hard and we have some *answers.*"

Fen's eyes grew wide with curiosity while Nar helped him spoon more soup into his famished body. "What answers?" was the question that blazed from Fen's eyes.

Charin sat next to Fen and began to fill him in on what had happened since he had collapsed. Finding out that the dilemma of Lars' reporting had been handled cleverly in a ruse, Fen began to rally.

"You've done great! You've all done exceptionally well and thank you for caring for me

– but what are the answers you and Gem have found?" he spoke softly, but intensely.

With one arm around Nar and the other around Gem's shoulder, Fen was able to stand and shuffle from the room. Light streamed in from the terrace through large windows in the cavernous living space, cheerful now in the late afternoon in spite of being mostly full of stacked boxes. Some of the boxes, however, had been unpacked hastily and then discarded.

They crossed into a large, richly-paneled study adjoining the terrace which had been set up for Charin to do research. Several tiers of screens and two consoles lined one wall with polished desks and expensive padded work chairs. The large windows to one side overlooked the terrace garden and landing pad. The cruiser still sat on the pad, but its terrifying "red stripe" had been restored.

"Well, I see we still have some 'Luck'," Fen said to Charin as he was helped to lower himself into one of the over-comfortable executive chairs.

Fen sat while Charin and alternately Gem told him what they had discovered.

"There is 'A Field' of unknown type that is permeating the surface of the planet," she began.

Charin, unable to account for her actions when Lars died, postulated: What if there were an unknown control placed upon her below her level of awareness? She tried to recall what in the environment might have set off such a mechanism and she remembered "The Plan." She told him of her "test" with Thara and the violent results. She was convinced that her reasoning was sound, so she went looking for "the field"... and she and Gem *found* IT!

Lars was apparently intending to set up a security control center here in the house and when they began to look into various boxes they found *tons* of equipment, most of which they would never normally have had access to.

What they found was staggering. The two orbiting lines of black pods they had lived with all of their lives were *not* placed for surveillance after the revolution – as they had been told – but *actively* broadcast some type of biologic field. Gem had discovered late one night when tracing various forms of radiation that a tiny amount of intermittant emissions seemed to be coming from *directly above.* After that, they recorded the traces and amplifying them noticed they seemed to contain a regular signal pattern, a clear sign of human origin. They concentrated their efforts on this very, very long band and...

Charin tapped a console key. There on the screens appeared hazy, slowly moving "dots" positioned in two bands moving in opposite directions with a "green" haze below them that became lighter as one scanned down the displays. The glow was most intense just below the "dots".

"There are the pods in orbit. You can clearly see that 'something' is being generated to flood the planet, and you can bet it's not doing us good." Charin finished.

# CHAPTER EIGHTEEN

## Calculated Move

"This is it!" Fen announced as Charin lightly touched "Luck" down at the foot of the steps to Temple. He kept pulling down on the waistband of Lars' somewhat ill-fitting scarlet uniform as he spoke — it was crucial, if uncomfortable, for him to look as much as possible a Senior Kill Corps officer.

Gem and Preed were also disguised. Preed, with his strong physique and dark helmet looked comfortably soldier-like in Krek's tight red uniform complete with snap-stick and boots. Gem, on the other hand with his slight build, wore maintenance blue and looked convincing as a city worker, with his yellow-helmet and sweaty forehead.

The rest of the crew were also outfitted for their tasks. Nar and Lall squirmed uncomfortably in their bulky pressure suits, holding their helmets in their laps, sitting in two oversize commando jumpseats that made them look like two cherub faces pressed into bulbous drinking mugs. In contrast, Charin's smooth fitting pressure suit emphasized her shape to advantage — she appeared ready for action as she sat at the pilot console.

Fen sighed and stopped fiddling with his waistband. It was time to rally everyone — he knew they all were depending upon him.

"You all know what we have to do and how long we have to do it. I can't say that we'll ever be together again, all of us, or we'll make it, but we have to try. If you have personal deities to whom your allegiance is given, invoke them now for our success! Now let's GO!"

Popping the hatch, Preed led the way pushing crowds to the side arrogantly. Fen haughtily walked a pace or two behind. Up the steps of Temple they marched trailed by Gem dragging an oversized maintenance cart behind him.

Charin wiped a tear from her cheek hoping Nar and Lall wouldn't see it — she and Fen had just said their private "goodbye." Now she was all business. She autosealed the hatch and piloted the cruiser, slowly ascending into the traffic lane.

Clearing the city lanes north of Capital, Charin slowly flew north following the coastline. They had picked a departure point on the border of a restricted military weapons testing zone. As her jump off to altitude would trigger alarms that would start the game and probably a mad chase, they figured that bureaucratic foul-ups between multiple testing outfits might give them an edge before officials figured out what was happening.

Fen and Charin had decided on this tactic because: The fact that no one had challenged Dactoes rulers directly in over a hundred years should work to their advantage due to official laziness and over-confidence. Charin hoped this wasn't just wishful thinking.

"Strap in!" she told Nar who had now moved to the weapons console.

"Now!" she said as they reached the restricted border, pushing the thrust levers to "max" and accelerating vertically as they were jammed down into their seats. "These things are supposed to be sub-orbital" a voice in Charin's head said as she gritted her teeth and grunted her breath so as not to black out.

**1st Voice:** "X6?" a loud voice in the cabin speaker sounded, "That you?"

**2nd Voice:** "What?"

**1st Voice:** (irritated) "I said, X6 is that you?!?"

**2nd Voice:** (irritated) "Yes it's me, what do you want?"

**1st Voice:** "You can't fly in this space without informing us! What test are you running and why haven't I been informed?"

**2nd Voice:** "You are out of your mind. I don't know what you are talking about."

**1st Voice:** "You just wait until your Group Leader hears about this infraction, we'll see who 'doesn't know what I'm talking about'!"

**2nd Voice:** "If Group Leader hears anything it will be about your incompetence!"

**1st Voice:** (yelling) "Switching to hard-line, OUT!"

Rising higher and higher into the sky, Charin felt waves of nausea pass through her body, as if they were physical punches. Despite this as the view screens darkened she was fascinated as the view cleared – STARS! Stars started to appear, not just the hazy white spots sometimes visible near the horizion at dawn or dusk, but real stars, twinkling white, some with a blue tinge, others with a slight yellow or red. She started to pull back the thrust as the target altitude was approaching. It would not do to overshoot or accidentially crash into an orbiting pod.

Suddenly, they were through. The wave haze was below them now like a sickly colored smoke but above, the bright stars shown like brilliant pin-pricks through a black roof, and Mother was a crisp, bright, crater-strewn beacon, seemingly within touch while Child hung sharp and crescent-shaped slightly above the distant horizon. The beauty and endlessness of the cosmos left Charin momentarily breathless. She felt her space expand and time slow down as her mind drifted from the purpose at hand. With great effort Charin wrenched herself back — but she would never forget that moment even if she never returned from this hopeless mission.

About a hundred clicks below them and crossing their course about twenty clicks ahead were two rows of counter rotating orbital pods. No longer fuzzy black dots, but grotesque great black "beans" of enormous size each sprouting "prickly" little pins with flat round plates at the ends — there were thousands of them.

There was an odd sensation Charin had never experienced before, a sort of lightness and clarity of thinking with brilliance of perception that seemed to permeate her. They had overshot their altitude target.

"Damn!" thought Charin, "And we have so little time to find the right two pods!"

"We're being scanned," said Nar.

Charin didn't waste a moment. Shooting the cruiser toward the orbiting pods and decending from above she paralleled their trajectory, hoping the pods would mess up the ground scans.

"Visitors. They are launching two battle wagons for us," said Nar grimly smiling, "ETA about forty minutes."

"Scan your screens, find the key pods, now! Lall. Nar, keep watching our visitors." Charin replied a cold sweat forming upon her brow.

All she could do now was wait. She reviewed the situation in her mind to calm her trembling nerves.

Once they had found out about the field being generated from the orbiting pods, they had begun a close study. At first all pods seemed identical, but further analysis showed that two pods were "special," one in each orbit. These pods did not put out the usual field signature, but instead seemed to have a horizontal output aligning along their orbit. Charin and Gem had guessed that these were the key control pods for all the others. Their entire plan was based upon this assumption.

They were betting their lives and the lives of everyone on the planet that this was true. Mapping the positions of the key pods, they had carefully calculated when the two oppositely orbiting key pods would be together on the same side of the planet (somewhere within reach of their stolen craft) hoping this would be before their tiny conspiracy was uncovered. Fortunately, this time was a matter of weeks, not months or years, so they set their timetable for action quickly. It was a desperate chance, sooner than they liked, but they had all agreed it was worth taking.

Charin pushed their cruiser to its limit to match the orbital velocity of the south-to-north pods. The two key pods should be approaching each other near them now. The pods were actually well under actual orbital velocity and slightly within the atmosphere. This indicated that each was artificially powered to hold their positions and not in free-fall. How this was done was unknown and appeared to be beyond the present state of Dactoes technology.

"Got 'em!" said Lall excitedly, spotting the key pods' positions and shocking Charin from her reverie.

"A third battle wagon is being dispatched," chanted Nar grimly.

The first "key" pod was in an excellent position relative to them. "Okay, Lall, get ready for your jump, I'll monitor the second key," said Charin.

It was probably a suicide mission, yet both Nar and Lall relished the prospect and volunteered immediately. The plan was to leave the cruiser in a pressure suit on a mini-spider thruster from above and descend to a key pod, disable it, then slowly descend with the spider through the wave cloud to a soft landing. Just because it had never been done and the chances were probably 100 to 1 of making it didn't slow them down a bit.

The immediate problem was they would have to decompress in order to open the cruiser hatch. (There was no air-lock in a craft never intended for off-planet operation.) Charin, Nar and Lall put on their helmets, checked seals and equalized pressure. Looking at each other with simply an acknowledging nod, Charin decompressed the interior and Lall opened the hatch.

The first launch went well. Lall landed his spider on the key, opened its hatch and waved a salute.

Now the race was really on. Charin had to reverse her course 180 degrees and try to match the opposite pod orbits. Although the second "key" pod had not yet arrived near their position, even at the cruiser's max thrust, the "key" would pass them by and they would have to catch up to it before Nar could exit. The flight deck began to heat as friction with the slight outside atmosphere built up.

"How long to catch the key?" Nar asked Charin.

"About eleven minutes." Charin gritted through the hard acceleration.

"How long until our first 'visitors' are within range?" she continued.

"About twelve minutes." Nar replied.

It would be very, very close. "I wonder what Fen is doing," she thought.

* * *

Fen walked purposefully through the crowd. Glancing over his shoulder he watched "Luck" rise into the traffic lane with a lump in his throat.

The concourse was not as busy as his previous visit, yet it was still with some trepidation he approached marker 66 along the pavement. This time, to his relief, he felt no disorientation or dizziness.

Gem began to set up the maintenance tent he dragged from his cart to cover the hexagonal pavement near marker 66. Water from a large barrel on the cart started to leak in a slow trickle from under the tent down the steps of the concourse, just enough to add a reason for the maintenance tent. Preed acted irritated at Gem and Fen acted irritated at Preed. Passers-by ignored them giving a wide berth to the red uniforms and water trickle. Domestic cop Lug was nowhere to be seen.

Gem found, as Fen had predicted, that the pavement was hinged as a hatch which opened when the right-sized rod was thrust into a small, nearly invisible hole near one edge. A ladder led below. Gem climbed down into a passageway about twenty feet below.

Checking around to make sure no one was watching, Preed and Fen entered the tent one by one. Preed climbed down the passageway first. Then Fen followed, closing the hatch behind him.

They were in.

* * *

Frake paced the High Dome, agitated. He had not been this apprehensive for over a hundred years. Where was that fool Lars?

"Women!" Frake fumed to himself. "These planetoid types are always so hormonal. Well Lars won't have the equipment to do anything about it unless that fool reports today."

Frake had put a full security alert into place about the High Temple for a week. To Frake's consternation nothing, absolutely nothing had happened, except for a report from Domestic that a top-ranking Kill Corps officer had appeared ill on his way to Temple and returned to his cruiser. Was that Lars?  Why had he not reported in via wrist band?

"Why can't we locate Lars' transponder? What is his game anyhow?  What *was* the meaning of the Seer's warning?" Frake began to pace even faster.

"Does Lars believe he could *actually* challenge *my* position?"

Frake never took chances with what could be a personal threat.  Walking to the Planetary console formulating a strategy, Frake cancelled the high alert, returning security to normal, opened a cabinet and personally armed himself as a precaution. "That fool Krek would greedily replace Lars," he thought as he dispatched a squad to Lars' home.  "I'll lure Lars in and rip out his plan bit by bit.  It will be pure pleasure to watch Lars twitch and scream as he dies."  A grim smile crossed Frake's countenance.

\* \* \*

Thara shuddered from the cold as she sat in a derelict patrol cruiser in the boneyard. "If only a power pack worked to heat up this dump," she thought pulling the thread-bare blanket tighter on her shoulders.

It had been a challenge relocating to the boneyard while guarding their three prisoners. They had become comfortable at Lars' place but Thara had pointed out, "We're all sitting ducks here. The new staff is due to show up and who knows what other squads of goonies Lars had in mind to watch this place." "We pulled off those desperate improvised 'dumb tricks' to delay the staff and cancel the 'bodyguards' once, but when do those ever work a second time?" she argued. The others had agreed and they spent four hectic days moving.

She tried not to think about the others. She tried not to think about Krek and the other two tied and bound in the tool locker, and how she might have to kill them and be the only rebel left if the others failed. She tried not to think about it but it was no use.

\* \* \*

The passage was narrow and unlit as Gem fumbled to unpack the infrared goggles and light from his pack. As he, Fen and Preed put them on, sight returned through a red haze. With Fen leading them, as though he knew where they were going, they navigated the constantly downward sloping passage stumbling occasionally over debris that had fallen from the ceiling but meeting no unpassable barriers.

The passage abruptly ended at a long wide room having several inches of water pooled on the floor. They seemed to be standing below a grating covering the ceiling which was part of the floor of a much, much larger space above. Splashing to the far wall, Fen found grooved handholds spaced like a ladder in the wall. Climbing this and pushing the covering grate to the side they emerged onto the floor of a pump room deep in the heart of Temple.

Following Fen without a word, they wound around the room up five series of stairs and through a dozen passages. Up and up they climbed. Finally Fen led them to a small room just large enough for three or four people. Stopping, he closed a thick door behind them and took off his goggles. There was a dim greenish glow from fluorescent floor strips they could see by.

"Interesting," he said, "For some reason – I'm not sure why, I seem to know all about this place. I know I've been here before. I had doubts before we came but now I'm certain."

Sitting down and motioning for the others to sit Fen checked the time then continued.

"Behind the panel I'm leaning on is a spiral stair that leads directly to Temple Dome. It's an escape route and unless there's a change, it won't have any security alarms." Fen paused, raising his eyebrows significantly, "No security alarms... because it has always been a secret."

"What will we find at the top?" interjected Preed.

"I don't know, but a hundred and fifty years ago it was the apartment of The Seer and also Planetary Control. The base of what is occurring on Dactoes must be here, all governmental orders come from Temple and the real rulers must be in or near High Dome, just as it has been for a thousand years. Check your gear, we should be prepared for anything."

With the others, Fen removed his snap-stick from its holder on his belt checking its charge. He took a second stick from Gem's pack and checking its charge fastened it with a strip to his left calf. He also picked three extra power modules from the pack and attached them to his belt with the first stick. Finally, he took a wrist torch from the pack and strapped it to his right wrist. The others were doing similar actions. Now, if there were a firefight they might have some chance of defending themselves.

They stood silent, nodding to each other. Fen pushed a corner of the panel he had been leaning against. It slid aside revealing the spiraling stair. "Just as I thought," Fen muttered to himself. With Fen leading, Gem followed and Preed brought up the rear. They began to climb.

It seemed interminable. Up and up and up they spiraled. There were no intermediate platforms, the stair just kept going. They climbed for about an hour, each step seeming heavier than the last until their backs and thighs ached and their breath came in grunts and still they climbed.

A sliver of light from somewhere above streaked across a wall barring their path as suddenly the stairs came to an abrupt halt on a small platform. Fen examined the wall and could clearly see it was a badly-built later addition. It didn't match the ancient construction of the stair and shaft and had been thrown on as an after-thought. Fen pointed his wrist torch to illuminate the scene while Gem carefully loosened some panel clips from a vertical support. With Preed pressing using the butt of his snap-stick they inched open a space large enough to crawl through one at a time.

They seemed to be in a storage closet. Fen found the door and after listening and hearing nothing slid it open a half inch. A finely panelled curved antechamber led away from the closet, very dimly lit. Fen somehow recognized it as the entrance to the Temple Dome. Pulling Lars' helmet from their pack and motioning the others to wait, Fen stepped into the antechamber placing the helmet on his head to hide his face, just in case.

Cautiously, Fen followed the curving wall to his right. As he approached the center of the antechamber he saw a large set of sliding panel doors standing open to his left and an equally large set of closed panel doors on his right, but these doors were intricately worked with a filigree of finely wrought symbols representing the ancient Regency of Dactoes and Office of The Seer. Fen was just about to decide which set of doors to take, when suddenly...

It was too late.

The outer doors slammed shut as the decorated inner doors suddenly opened in a flash. There stood a huge man, twelve-foot tall, handsomely proportioned but immense. Standing behind a tall console in close-fitting red, wearing a uniform that outlined his well-toned musculature, the hulk looked straight ahead, directly into Fen's eyes.

Fen's hidden helmeted face was staring right at the man's belt.

Clearly startled but recovering instantly, Frake cynically said, "LARS! Where in hell have you been?"

# CHAPTER NINETEEN

## Answers

Frake thought furiously. Who had Lars bribed to gain unannounced entry? Where did the funds come from? What members of his own personal guards were in on it? If he sounded the silent "general alarm" would it instantly be himself against a dozen others? Better to handle Lars one-on-one. He chuckled to himself recalling his caution to personally arm himself. He could handle Lars. Let the drama play on and see if he could uncover the other conspirators so he could enjoy carving them up bit by bit listening to their screams before he started on Lars.

Fen thought furiously. This *had* to be Frake — and Frake was an alien! Clearly humanoid, but some skeletal proportions did not seem quite right. Behind him reclining on a couch in the center of a huge circular depression matching the arched dome some forty feet overhead, sat an ancient human. He was clothed in grey robes that came close to matching the color of his wizened skin. A series of tubes protruded through the robe in places disappearing into the couch. This had to be The Seer — and he was a prisoner.

"Sick." Fen croaked in a scratchy imition of Lars voice as he took several steps into the dome while closely watching Frake's hands and demeanor.

141

Frake started laughing, "Sick? I'm a fool if you think I'd believe that. I've been trying to get a transponder fix on you for days — how did you find it and turn it off? Who's behind you?"

Fen automatically placed his feet in a defense posture and quickly whipped his snap-stick from behind him on his belt pointing it at Frake.

"Don't make any quick movements and keep your hands off of the console where I can see them," ordered Fen.

Frake continued to laugh and focusing his attention on Fen said, "You weak-minded humans haven't a chance. You *dare* to challenge *ME!*"

Fen stared as a distortion started to form in front of Frake, the air shimmered and the air seemed to coalesce. A blast of force hit Fen squarely in the chest, followed by a wave of nausea. He was prepared instinctively for this but it shook him all the same.

Looming in front of him was the burning, churning creature — Frake!

At last Fen knew: He knew who he was, who he had been, what he had been fighting for. Ripping the helmet from his head with his free hand he thought and said aloud in a strange, strong voice that was not himself yet was more himself at the same time: "Get the hell out of my way! Fiend!"

"YOU!" Frake screamed and a pain shot through Fen's head as though it were being crushed in a vise.

Fen dropped to his knees and tried to fire the snap-stick — but his hand refused his command and remained immobile. Fen fought back in this battle of wills. "KRAK!!" the snap-stick fired wild, blowing a gaping hole in a portion of panel just below the dome. Frake's deep-toned, evil laugh rose to a howl of glee.

Then slowly, Fen's hand and arm of their own accord started raising his snap-stick to point toward his own head. Dizzyness ran through his head, the pain increased and he wobbled on his knees. As Fen helplessly watched, Frake reached to his thigh and pulled his own snap-stick, puny in his huge hand, and pointed it at Fen.

Despite desperately fighting his paralysis, Fen could feel his trembling finger start to pull on the trigger of his own stick pointing at his head.

Just then, two blasts fired from the doorway almost simultaneously. One knocked Fen's stick from his hand just as the trigger closed, blasting a hole into the floor. The other blast took out Frake's stick and his right hand up to the wrist.

Running into the chamber Gem and Preed prepared to fire again. Fen felt the force holding him waver in strength, sometimes overpowering, sometimes faint. Suddenly both Gem and Preed dropped screaming to the floor and to all appearances were dead.

"Racktar Plen!" Fen grunted through his pain.

Frake's massive frame lumbered over to Fen, hovering over him. He wasn't laughing now.

"You know my name? Anyone who knows the name of The Racktar *and* can say it are too dangerous to live. I'm through fooling with you, human. Watch now as your flesh explodes!"

Fen felt a tension starting along his cheeks and spreading from his face down his chest. He fell back from his knees onto his heels. He had failed. How cocky he'd been to think he could win, but now his friends were dead, all of them probably by now. They had trusted him and he had led them to certain death. He willed himself to die.. but somehow it would not happen.

Just then there was an immense "pop" as if the whole universe had suddenly changed.

All of the tension and pain in Fen disappeared, in fact, he felt lighter than he had in his entire life. Fen concentrated all of his pent-up intensity upon Frake. The distortion that was Frake started to disperse, first as a cloud then as a fog then a mist and finally the body itself. Frake physically seemed to shrivel and crumble as his age, hundreds of years old, began to reveal itself. His body tumbled across the lower part of the Planetary Console, smoking and shrinking further as it fell.

Across the room a weak ancient voice asked, "When is it? When is now?" The Seer was sitting propped on an elbow and a slight color was flushing his chalklike cheeks.

Fen heard a groan and turned. Gem was lying on his back breathing hard and rubbing his head but alive! Preed was still out, but Fen could see him breathing although he had a nasty cut across his forehead. There was a bouyant optimism now bubbling through Fen. He helped Gem shakily to stand, smiling as he thought of the "hero's scar" Preed would show his grandchildren.

Hobbling to the Planetary Console, Gem activated it. "12B13tarbell" the Seer told him, "it's the password." he said with an ancient smile.

"They've done it! They've done it! They've disabled the pods, the field is down!" Gem cried.

# CHAPTER TWENTY

## Cleanup

The weeks that followed were hectic but amazing. It seemed a heavy weight had been removed from the entire planet populace following the powering off of the orbiting pods. Formerly disagreeable clans seemed happy to cooperate with each other.

Fen buried himself in reorganization. He and Gem located the leader of the Council, Jaytee who had been arrested by Krek for treason and had him released and escorted to Temple Dome. After fully briefing him on the Dactoes situation, the fact that the head of Kill Corps was in fact an alien and that other aliens were enroute to arrive within 100 years and wipe the planet clean of humans or enslave them. Once things were somewhat ordered, Fen turned over Planetary Control to Jaytee. Not too suprisingly (except to Fen) Jaytee named Fen Dathrod of Clan Grem the new Seer.

With the cleanup in minister Jaytee's hands, Fen was extremely anxious to find out what happened to the rest of his team. Thara was the easiest, as she was where she was expected to be. Krek and the goonies were arrested and Thara, fiery as ever, was just glad to have a hot bath and be free of Krek and the temptation to shoot him. In the end, she taped his mouth both to her relief and the other prisoner goonies.

Preed cleaned up well, and as the New Seer had predicted, was very, very proud of his "battle scar" stiched across his forehead.

Lall had done it: Disabled his orbit of pods with no difficulty and descended via the rickety spider craft slowly through the wave haze over two hours to land inland on Tarpin, ditch his pressure suit then fly his spider to the coast to lose himself on a beach. Unsure what to do, Lall was planning to fly back to Capital in a long series of short hops when Fen found him.

Nar had had a rough time. Charin had dropped him to his pod in the nick of time before she ran from the two pursuing battle cruisers dodging their blasts while ignoring their orders to stand down. It was tricky for him. He wanted to be sure to disable his line of orbiting pods at or near the same time as Lall because there might have been a cross connection. He also was not sure he was unseen dropping from their cruiser to the pod so he felt time might be running out. He rigged his pod then waited. In the end, both he and Lall disabled nearly simultaneously.

When he went to begin his tricky descent, he found his spider had been damaged when he alighted the key pod. After two days, with his oxygen running low, he managed to get the spider (mostly) working. Somehow he kept the craft together for a four hour tortuous drop in crazy spirals and zooms to a crash landing in Tarf's bomb-cratered back country.

Nar had broken his shoulder in the landing then almost died hiking to the nearest town where he was hospitalized. That was where Fen finally located him.

No trace of Charin had turned up. Fen hoped his "luck" had not run out.

# CHAPTER TWENTY·ONE

## At Last

Charin was the hardest. Fen could not find out what had happened to her nor whether she was still alive. He tried again and again not to think about what losing her might mean to him. Nar had told Fen of the firefight and dance in the sky and Charin's brilliant piloting. Fen found and talked with the commanders of all three battle cruisers dispatched to chase her. All three told him their orders were to capture the craft, not destroy it. Despite numerous stunning blows she had still managed to elude them and the craft had simply disappeared. With despondent heart, Fen tried reading reports of sightings, crashes, any unusual event. He had a sinking feeling Charin may have gone down into the sea.

Each night, late into the night, Fen sat over his terminal at Temple in minister Jaytee's and his shared office searching for Charin and losing hope.

One unexpected change brought by the disassembling of the orbital pods and field was that the "wave cloud" – something Fen and everyone for generations had come to believe was a natural phenomena – began to disperse.

Each day dawned brighter with the sky having a blue-green tinge, but each night more and more stars started to be visible until the vast cosmos was revealed in awesome display. It was amazing how everyone would simply go out night after night and *look* at the sky, and far from feeling smaller and insignificant they would somehow feel *bigger* for having survived.

Fen pushed back from his desk in the dark office and walked to the newly installed large window to simply gaze at the sky. "How beautiful it is," he thought. Suddenly something even more beautiful ripped his attention away from the starscape, Charin walked in!

His emotion was so intense he didn't know what to do. He stood numb and dumb as she walked over to him with a big smile.

Quietly she sauntered over to his side and holding his left arm gently in her hands said, "I landed off the coast in the sea, had to swim for it. When I made the beach I had nothing. Domestic Police picked me up as a vagrant and possible prostitute. I've been in jail, 'fraid I have a criminal record now to add to rebel among other things. You might not want me back," she bantered.

Fen didn't speak. Together they looked out the window at the stars with a beautiful, clear crescent Child slowly rising above the horizon. Tears ran down Fen's cheeks in the silence as Charin leaned her head on Fen's shoulder.

Minister Jaytee came from his office and walked to where they were standing. Smiling slightly toward Charin, without a word he too stood next to Fen and looked out.

"Is this your consort, Fen?" asked minister Jaytee nodding toward Charin who flushed and averted her eyes for a second.

"Yes!" Charin said with a huge smile as she clasped Fen's hand in hers stepping up even closer beside him, "Yes I am, Dad!" It was Fen's turn to blush.

## ∗∗ Finis ∗∗